The Fishfly

Robert Maniscalco

PublishAmerica
Baltimore

© 2005 by Robert Maniscalco.

All rights reserved. No part of this book may be reproduced, stored in a retrieval system or transmitted in any form or by any means without the prior written permission of the publishers, except by a reviewer who may quote brief passages in a review to be printed in a newspaper, magazine or journal.

First printing

Cover art by Robert Maniscalco, entitled "Deliquesence"
Cover design by Yael Edelstein

ISBN: 1-4137-4184-3
PUBLISHED BY
PUBLISHAMERICA, LLLP.
www.publishamerica.com
Baltimore

Printed in the United States of America

The Fishfly is dedicated to my parents, family and friends, who have inspired me and challenged me to grow and discover my connection with humanity. Also, to my amazing wife, Amanda, who has given me the luxury of time, space and encouragement needed to complete this book. And finally, to Daniel, my son, who is here to teach me about love and what it really means to be human.

Special thanks also go to those dear ones who have taken the time to give me the honest feedback and encouragement necessary to bring *The Fishfly* into being: Mirjanna Urosev, James Maniscalco, Ann Kennedy, Tova Salinger, Jan Titsworth, Joe Ales, Kristi Watterberg, Joan Laurence, Miriam Engstrom, Kay Maniscalco and my editor, Don Harvey.

PRELUDE

THERE ARE TWO DOORS LEADING TO my freedom. One is slightly ajar, the other locked shut, with lots of stuff piled up in front of it. My stuff. As always, I choose the door with all the stuff in the way. I figure, there's got to be something pretty amazing behind door number two. Where's Bob Barker when you need him?

This dream morphs into the one where I'm being found guilty of murder. Sometimes I escape from prison. Sometimes I'm executed. Always I wake up. Someday I won't.

I suppose I should consider myself lucky to be awake now, under the circumstances. But am I *lucky* to be awake or is there a higher power at work? How is it I'm still alive at all? Is it really true that because I think, therefore I am? Am I, really? And if I didn't, would I not be? Is ours simply but to do? Or is it just to be? At what point does a thought become action? And when do actions become destiny?

Sometimes, I don't know which I prefer least, being asleep or awake.

Chapter 1
8:37 a.m. - Ash Wednesday

AS FAR AS I CAN TELL, in my waking stupor, my mission here remains intact. The New Orleans sun sears its way through the bleached sheers of a towering, arched window. Pinning my left arm to the mattress is a woman—a girl, really. *Where did she come from? Why should it matter, jerk?* Is my arm asleep? *Who cares!* The squabbles have begun in earnest. There is no rest from the voices in my head, asleep or awake.

The girl nuzzles up to my chest, breaking the delicate string of drool that seems to have been connecting our souls. The full weight of her head rests, now, over my heart, like the Bronze Medal of Honor. The stillness of this moment has a serene yet implausible nobility to it.

Across the room my pale linen suit is strewn over the back of a freshly gilded, antique chaise lounge. Why does linen wrinkle so easily? *Where am I?* the groggy voice of alarm mumbles into my ear. *This isn't part of the plan, you idiot,* comes the strident voice of judgment. It's true; my mission did not include this particular encounter. *You think you're so clever, Mr. Studman,* inserts the familiar voice of emasculation. *Can't you do anything right?*

Stop!

The humidity and dust in the air create a veil of nostalgia over the clutter of antiques and densely hung paintings, loosely covered by white cotton cloths—not sheets. The room looks more like a museum warehouse than any kind of a bedroom. *What are you doing here?* barks the impatient voice of judgment once again. *You're way off track.* I know. *Why couldn't you stick to the plan?* I'm sorry. *You never finish what you start! You're here to do murder not sleep with strange women.*

Shut up! I know why I'm here.

Last night is a blur. I remember arriving at the airport and being shoved into a shuttle bus. The driver hauled us as close to downtown New Orleans as he dared. It was Mardi Gras, after all.

The traffic slowed to a halt where I-10 stands at eye level with the downtown skyline. I said to the driver, "Ten bucks if you stop this thing and open the door." There was no response. My claustrophobia was kicking in so I decided to turn my mild nausea into an Academy Award-winning performance of dry heaves. I thought I was very convincing.

Finally he muttered, "It's against the rules, asshole." I hate people who talk to you with toothpicks in their mouths. Eventually, we made it all the way to the St. Charles Hotel, on the edge of the French Quarter. "Welcome to the Big Easy. Now get the fuck out."

I stepped out into the thick sprawl of people. There were no cars anywhere, just a multitude of crushing resolve. I moved with the crowd. As we got closer to the French Quarter it became so dense that the surge of humanity began to sway in drunken lunges under its own weight. I didn't fight it. It wasn't any worse than the Lexington Avenue subway platform at rush

THE FISHFLY

hour. But unlike those in the New York subway, these people weren't trying to get somewhere else. We were all here because we wanted to be, here at the epicenter of iniquity. This is where people go when they want to pretend to be bad, where they can indulge in a little harmless moral relaxation—the perfect cover for some real mischief.

Even though I had no idea where this crowd was taking me, I had the distinct feeling that *it* did. There's an intelligence in crowds. It was as if some great machine was pulling me into its maw. Like the Planet Killer from *Star Trek*'s "Doomsday Machine," which nearly sucked the Enterprise into its great furnace of oblivion, I was being pulled by a tractor beam into the sewer of the French Quarter.

Getting to PJ's was out of the question. I had hooked up with her a few weeks before, through an on-line arts forum back in New York. We'd been e-mailing back and forth ever since. My plan was to stay with PJ last night. But plans change. Or get modified.

Nothing to worry about, comes the soft, barely audible voice of reassurance. *What are you talking about? You've gotten yourself way off track*, blasts the bully.

I had no idea where to find PJ's flat and no way of getting there if I could. I'd probably have to explain to her where I'd been last night. *What's to explain, asshole? Something better came along. You don't owe her anything*, the bully bellowed. *You've jeopardized the whole mission over a one-night stand*, came the graveled, desperate voice of *Star Trek*'s Dr. McCoy. Captain Kirk and Spock are in there too, along with a long cast of other players, friends and foes, real and imagined, all competing for precious brain time.

Allow me to explain. I hear voices in my head. It's not like I hallucinate or anything. I'm not psychotic, really. Still, I was always afraid to answer, "yes" on those psychological tests asking whether you hear voices. I figure everyone hears voices. *They're called thoughts, asshole*. Yes, but maybe mine are just a little more distinct, more animated than most. *How would you know, you've never been in anyone else's head.* I didn't want my shrinks to think I was crazy, like real crazy, even though I probably was—I mean, am.

Anyway, the point is, I don't remember seeing a pay phone the whole night. So there was no way I could have called her. *Don't give me any of your goddamn excuses,* blurts another voice, now beginning to sound very much like Captain Kirk. Or was that my father. Sometimes the voices get jumbled. *You're the one that's jumbled. The trouble with you is you have the will to fail. You're a big nothing.* Okay. That's definitely my dad's voice.

It was around 8:30 p.m. last night when I'd achieved an involuntary oneness with the collective hordes. Like the Borg, I began to realize, "resistance was futile." Did I mention, *Star Trek* was my primary formative authority?

Since it was Mardi Gras I felt justified in having my first drink in a year. Actually, I really needed it. Feelings of awe and dread, which are the telltale signs of an existential crisis, were beginning to build and that needed a drink. I think I remember hearing someone mention that the drive-through frozen daiquiri stands down here had been open since five a.m. One of a myriad of enigmas in a place someone else referred to as, "the Big Sleazy."

The whole town was thick with the mud made from a grotesque variety of spilled beer and incomprehensible alcoholic combinations vomited here and there. Add to that the hodgepodge of squeals, grunts, flashes of light and personal odors and it was truly an obscene sensory orgy. The chaos was just what I'd hoped it would be. After all, I didn't come down here for a good time, or to *pretend* to be naughty. No, I've come down here with a definite purpose, one best accomplished beneath the veil of confusion. What better place to find or lose oneself? What better opportunity to commit a murder?

THE FISHFLY

Around 9:30 the crowd ejaculated me into a small pocket of breathable air just off Royal Street. The slightly thinner crowd gave me a chance to escape from the insanity of the moment. I took out my sketchbook and began to draw. It goes with me everywhere. It's a force of habit. Like the briefcase connecting the president to his weapons of mass destruction, our doomsday machine. My sketchbook is an old friend.

Last night I sketched anything I saw: costumes, flying beads, women's breasts, lost souls, carefree souls. Soon there was a crush of people again, staring, groping, pressing against one another, as if they were fighting over the same molecules of putrid air. Amazingly, through all the commotion, in my own quiet way, I had created a stir with just the ink from my pen. People began clambering to see what I was doing.

It was then I saw her, the girl, the one asleep beside me now, wearing a particularly loose body drape, so white it was almost blue, as she brushed past me. I'd say she was maybe twenty-five. I remembered seeing her on the airport shuttle which dropped me off near the hotel. *She must have gotten caught up in the same energy flux that brought you to this place and time.* What are the odds of that? *About 6,327 to 1. Shut up, Spock, I'm sick of your half-breed interference!*

Was her appearance an amazing coincidence or was she actually following me for some reason? *Don't be such a jerk. Why would she follow you? What would be the point?*

I sometimes wonder if inner voices should be allowed to argue among themselves or ask rhetorical questions. *Why shouldn't they?* These are the debates I hate. The only time these voices stop is when I draw.

I remember her smell as she passed: oil of cloves. I know it well. I used to put a drop or two in my oil paints to keep them from drying out too fast. It made them smell good too. Perhaps that explains why she seemed familiar to me. I wonder if she's one of those girls who smoke clove cigarettes. It's about the worst thing you can possibly do to your body—fatalistic, yet somehow erotic.

She didn't try to catch my eye. She didn't have to. It was as if we were alone in the midst of the befuddled crowd.

I remember filling page after page of my sketchbook. She must have known I was drawing her. She seemed chic and aloof, like she was toying with me. But it was clear she was enjoying the attention.

As my eye moved, so did my pen, in tandem with her body. Okay, I admit it. I found myself hoping for a glimpse of her sweet forbiddens. *What a pervert! You're such a freak!* Yes, I know. So tacky, and I've worked so hard to stay above the fray. And then, in a series of graceful gestures she exposed a subtle variety of private parts in fleeting revelations. She seemed to stumble, then barely recover her balance, turning herself into a whirl of continuous movement. The sweet, shadowy curve of a breast met with its resting place on her chest. In an instant she seemed to step through the safety of her wrap and then back again, in a kind of controlled vulnerability. Her erotic dance was both sophisticated and imaginative.

She rose above the myriad of pretty young college coeds, milling around her, who were behaving as if they'd just escaped from a Pepsi Generation commercial. They meandered, mindlessly yet predictably, like schools of fish darting in tandem. A strawberry blond girl giggled, as she flipped open her shirt, mechanically brandishing her pert breasts. It was as if one of those awful *Girls Gone Wild* videos had come grotesquely to life. *How would you know, you've only seen the commercials!*

There were breasts everywhere I looked. I tried not to. Some were small, some were large, some were tattooed, some pierced. The girls displayed their wares in exchange for tangled strings of worthless plastic beads, tit for tat, so to speak. The boys haggled with the girls, their eyes groping voraciously for more flashes of flesh, trying to pretend it was only a game. Their low moans were barely audible under the whoops and screams erupting from the throngs. What a barbaric ritual. I wonder how the anthropologists, five hundred years from now, will explain it.

Whatever their motives, they clearly were part of the moment at hand. She and I weren't. My pen took down every nuance as she made a blue-white whirl in the light. We seemed to have an understanding, a rapport. It was as if we recognized something in one another—an inexplicable familiarity. What was it? My pen seemed to understand it even if I didn't. Was it because I'd seen her earlier? Maybe I just recognized her expression of pathos, her hurt, her knowing. It was all there in black and white, recorded in the rhythm of my lines: each drawing was an expression of her desire to be free. Free from what, I wondered.

The light of flaming torches, carried by a sweaty procession of bare-chested young black men marching to clanging cowbells, shimmered on the forms of her relinquishment to the moment. The flambeaux carriers, bearing bulky propane beasts upon their backs, seemed so proud and regal, yet ever mindful of the tossed coin. Their nostrils flared. Musky perspiration poured onto the streets, leaving a pungent trail of absurdity.

But for us there were no words, only the poetry of lines. My drawings became the psychological blueprint of our combined inner turmoil and self-awareness, hidden beneath and expressed through the drapery of her thin white raiment. It was as if each quivering movement was a response to my lines. Her strength, her pain, her soul were transformed into form on page after page of my sketchbook.

Occasionally, when I've wielded my pen, the living dead around me have become curious. But this time, as I drew the girl, I began to feel a marveling in the crowd more intense than ever before. *Fascinating, Captain, it's like nothing we've encountered before. Shut up, Spock!* People were pushing in on me, elbowing one another, struggling for a glimpse of my sketches.

"Hey, dude, draw me, man."

"Lemme see what you're drawing."

"Hey, check this dude out. This guy's drawing that chick over there."

Some among them seemed to be fighting to give me space, while others only pushed in to see what I was doing. It was as if they were responding to a deep need in the air for something truly extraordinary to happen. As for me, I only saw the trail of her lines moving through space.

This is my one true gift, my dharma. I'm exceptional in my ability with a line. I can't control or explain the movement of the hand or what I'm doing when I draw. My hand has the intelligence of a river; the current knows where it is going. The gift has never failed me, though I must admit this was the first time it had ever persuaded a girl to go to bed with me. *Male chauvinist pig!* Oh, hi, Mom.

Ordinarily, I would have been content to play the fool, to walk away knowing I had made the spiritual connection and leave the conquest to someone else. I'd never been with a woman who fucked a man with resolve. Frankly, I resent that I've spent my whole life trying to improve myself, developing my sensitivities, my talents, my integrity, only to have some other guy come along at two a.m. and take home the beautiful woman with whom I've been developing a spiritual connection since eleven. Why do women always go home with the guys who are too stupid to consider what assholes they are?

No, I'd never gotten "lucky" with a woman. That is until last night. She came to me as if by magic. There were no words. She led me by the hand down the crowded streets through the back entrance of some kind of an antique store. I think. It was dark. Muted screams emanated from the streets. A marble Madonna blessed us from her pedestal as we passed.

I'm not sure I remember what happened after that. I don't recall actually making love to her, not in the way most people think of a man and woman making love, you know, sexually. I don't remember, for instance, ever removing my pants. In fact, I'm still wearing them. *What kind of a conquest was that?* barks the voice of emasculation. *Must have been a pity fuck.* Either way, my plans for last night didn't include this. Although it sure beats the hell out of murder.

Chapter 2
9:08 a.m.

MY ARM IS DEFINITELY ASLEEP. I wonder if she's really out cold or if she's just faking it. *That's illogical. Why would she pretend to be asleep?* comes the passive-aggressive voice of Mr. Spock again. Is she hoping I'll leave or is it an invitation to stay? *Maybe she's just tired.*

I have to decide, either chew my arm off at the shoulder, coyote-like, or risk waking her. Stealthily, I slide my arm out from under her. *You clumsy jerk, don't wake her up,* chides Dr. McCoy from my shoulder. In one motion, she rolls from her side onto her back, exposing her soft underbelly.

I stop breathing. *Oh God, she's beautiful.* I wait. *What are you doing, you freak?* I'm waiting. *What are you waiting for?* I think she's asleep. Her breasts are perfectly symmetrical. *A rare occurrence in human females. Shut up, Spock!* Her skin is like a baby's; a silky membrane of milky glazes form a delicate layer over her belly and thighs.

Slowly, quietly, I reach down into the canvas bag containing everything I own in the world. I pull out my Palm Pilot and silently fire it up, reviewing the last paragraph I wrote in my journal, yesterday, on the plane down here from New York:

> *I'll be the first to admit that life hasn't been what I'd hoped it would be when I was in heaven looking down on this poor world, thinking how much better I could do if only given half the opportunity. Having now had half the opportunity...let me put it this way: I've become fluent in several anguishes. I have picked at my life like a scab. This is my reality. This has always been my reality.*

I backspace and resume writing with my handy stylus:

> *This had always been my reality—until now. I believe I have found the missing link between my past and present. Being in action has made all things possible, even getting lucky. Now for the first time in my life I feel ready to step through to the other side of my longing, into my destiny. I stop. I inhale the life—my life—which has brought me to this threshold.*

What a bunch of malarkey, interrupts the raspy voice of my father. Thanks, Dad, thanks for the critique. He's right, though. My writing is contrived. Journals just don't do my experiences justice. I've often wondered what would happen if I could actually write down every thought I had over the period of one day. What would that look like? I turn off the Palm and put it away.

    The sunlight paints her form like a Vermeer. I lean toward her on one elbow. Keeping my fingers as close to her skin as I can without actually touching her, I slowly move my hand back and forth, down past her stomach, up and over the elegant curves of her breasts. I can feel her energy through my fingertips. I feel her pain, like a Vulcan. Her skin bristles with a magnetic softness, pulling at my hand. Her hair, freshly banged and black, frames her sweet face as it spills downward over her shoulders onto her pillow.

I wish I could recall more of what happened after the mad sketching of last night, after climbing the stairs to this room. One thing I definitely remember is the reason I'd given up drinking. It's very disturbing that I can't seem to remember large passages of last evening.

I do remember laughing. We laughed a lot. In fact, my stomach is sore. I haven't laughed like that in a long time. She said something about feeling safe with me. *She probably thought you were a faggot,* comes another old but familiar voice from my shoulder: that's the voice of Russ, my very first friend, the king of crass.

I vaguely remember rubbing her shoulders and neck. She seemed to devour my touch. She fell asleep and I put her to bed. Her white raiment must have slid off in her sleep. I don't remember removing it. Did she? I wonder.

To be in bed with such an attractive young woman—it's hard to believe. What would Captain Kirk do? *Energize, Mr. Scott.* No, I don't think so. *Such men dare take what they want.* He'd have had her first, *then* remember his obligation to his ship. Will I ever learn?

Actually, I've grown content to watch from afar. In fact, I've come to prefer it. As an artist I'd made a career out of observing, studying the human form, noticing things—detached. To be an artist is to be a voyeur, which makes it the loneliest, most private form of human expression. When I think of the hours I've logged drawing the nude model in sketch classes…I'm sure I'd be the envy of every junior high school basketball team in the country.

Of course my art was more than simple voyeurism. I was an observer of life. I've learned to pay attention. I've sketched in restaurants, shopping malls, and convalescent homes. Airports are the best. My gift was for simple, honest observation,

THE FISHFLY

responding to what was seen and felt before me. It's a skill that is no longer valued in our post-modern, cynical society.

Back when I lived in New York City, I used to sit for hours and draw the people in the many windows of the building across the alley from my apartment. They were my friends, my city-mates, each in their private worlds, in their respective compartments—like *Hollywood Squares*, minus the chitchat. Over the years I had sketched them in every imaginable variation of daily activity. Sometimes I just watched. Eventually, it was as if I were part of their families—their lives. I saw them fight, watch TV, gain and lose weight, eat, bathe, work at their computers, ride their stationary bikes and, of course, fuck, suck and masturbate. But mainly I just watched them be. I considered it an honor to be a part of their lives. *I doubt they felt the same about you, you pervert.* True, there's a certain amorality in being an artist. Sometimes a vision must be stolen; sacrifices must be made for a higher purpose.

What is her name? a voice inside me interrupts. *It doesn't matter,* snaps another. *Why spoil this perfectly wonderful encounter with names and numbers no one gives a shit about anyway?* I take a deep breath. Whose voice was that? I can't keep track.

The precipitation between her breasts glistens as the sunlight cuts a textured pattern through the satin sheers, across her body, accentuating her extraordinary topography. She is spread beside me now, sheet-less against the heat, her legs opened, invitingly. *She wants it. They all do.* Shut up, Russ, that's disgusting. Nevertheless, I move down over her, very slowly.

I've never seen anyone enjoy her sleep so much. She's like a puppy. Carefully, without touching, I nuzzle into the nest I've created within the arch of her slightly out-turned left leg. My face is positioned directly above the epicenter of male longing.

That scent—it's faint but unmistakable. I never understood how men could be so crass as to compare this glorious aroma to anything inhuman. But for some reason, here in the darkness between her sweet white legs, I recall the fairy-winged fishflies: those harmless, likeable bugs from my youth. The fishflies came in swarms, in early summer, in a small region around Lake Saint Clair, just outside Detroit, where I grew up. Born without stomachs, they live only for a day and smell, well, like fish.

The scent brings back the agony of my furtive experiences between the legs of my first real girlfriend. Her name I will never forget. Jami was my high-school sweetheart. She dotted the "i" in her name with a heart. We didn't believe in premarital sex. Okay, the truth is I didn't believe in it because she didn't. By this time I was a back-slidden Pentecostal. And even though religion had failed me years before I was not yet ready to admit it to anyone but God.

It's ironic that I should think about that now. After all, what is a "sin," to someone as far gone as I? After all, sins are forgivable; alienation is much trickier. It's kind of absurd to be pondering the "wages" of premarital sex when you're a man of forty-four, *who's planning to commit a murder, for God's sake.*

But as a sixteen-year-old, Jami wanted so much to be good. And at seventeen, I wanted so much to be good in Jami's eyes. She came into my life soon after my relocation to Bloomfield Hills, an affluent suburb northwest of Detroit. My father, who had always aspired to the "good life," had just married a wealthy heiress. Now he was living the life he'd always dreamed: clean, organized, splendid. His "ship had finally landed," as he described it. For me, the whole arrangement was a complete culture shock. I had no socioeconomic aspirations beyond the middle-class suburb in which I'd grown up. Other people were rich, not me.

I was incredibly homesick and desperately needing to belong. Jami provided me with a fleeting glimpse of companionship in this strange new world. My step-family seemed neither willing nor able to make me feel welcome. And

I hadn't yet learned how to do this for myself.

When we moved it was like a light switch turned off. Suddenly, I was the outsider in my own home. The day he remarried, my father sat me down and told me, "I'm sorry, Donny, I want to make this perfectly clear: you're no longer going to be number one in my life. We're committed to making this marriage work," he told me, assertively. "This is Brenda and Melissa's home. From now on we do things their way."

Melissa was Brenda's daughter. She didn't go to school. She hung out in her room with the self-assuredness of someone who knew they'd never have to work for a living. She read a lot and kept mostly to herself. Apparently, Melissa had experienced some unspeakable trauma which prevented her from going out in public. I'd heard gunplay was involved. Her psychiatrist got her addicted to Valium when she was ten, to calm her nerves. Although she seemed perfectly charming on the surface I sensed a deep sadness to which I had no access.

My other step-siblings were off at college and rarely visited. Meals consisted of pleasant, though sparse conversation, with the occasional kick under the table from my father if I fell asleep between courses or said the wrong thing. In short, I was tolerated but never embraced. My home life was a microcosm for class relations everywhere.

They made a bedroom for me in what had been their billiards room. Now, instead of the pool table, they were stuck with me. It was like *Cinderella*, without the Fairy Godmother. My room had no windows. It was furnished like a Super 8 Motel. Even the pictures were nailed to the walls. It was the fitting consummation of a failed adolescence.

Jami became my only refuge. I remember the times when our passions would become overly sexual. My mouth would find its way "down there" and she would invariably twist away like a pearl diver running out of air, gasping to reach the surface of a deep, dark lagoon, not wanting to hurt my feelings. It was all part of her delicious morality dance.

It was the sweetest of agonies, to be groping guiltily under the dashboard of my father's car or on the sawdust floors of half-built homes without ever getting to share my deepest expressions of sexual pleasure with the only girl I would ever love. By that time I had accepted the ache of rejection that was to become the running monologue of my life. Jami and I abstained from sex in the name of Jesus Christ, who died on the cross for our sins almost two thousand years ago. Small consolation for a horny teenager. Why did premarital sex have to be a sin? How could physical redemption be so wrong? I'm convinced it is the one act that could have freed me from the prison of alienation and dread in which I was living. Talk about blue balls!

Instead, I had to teach myself to be satisfied with the delightful little tastes Jami would offer me on occasion. That was her one true gift to me: the sense memory of what *might* have been. It consisted of the faint odor of fishflies, mixed with Jontue perfume and Shower to Shower baby powder. To this day, it is the perfect combination of aromas.

At the end of my senior year, Jami and I came to a decision that it would be best for us to break up. She was going to be a senior in the fall and I would be starting music school at Wayne State University—over forty miles away. It's hard to believe how far that seemed, considering the distances I've traveled since. It seemed to make sense back then. "We'd be living in two entirely separate worlds." "Life was leading us in different directions." "To everything there is a season." I made proper use of all the usual clichés people invoke to justify "our self-made purgatories," as Mr. Spock once called them.

On our last date she gave me a small cardboard box wrapped in silver paper, into which she had placed little remembrances of our love. Among them, a strawberry blond lock of her hair, a photo of her as a little girl getting ready for her first boyfriend—which turned out to be me, a Bumble Bee refrigerator magnet to remind me of the time we almost got stung while making out in the woods of Echo Park, and a swatch of satin from a blouse she had made herself and which I had briefly removed to reveal her delicate breasts.

So here's my question: if God so loved the world, why wouldn't He let me go all the way with Jami?

Silence.

Why is it that the only time I ever hear silence in my head is when I address God directly? He never seems to answer the really important questions. I guess that's how He keeps us mortals hanging on.

The girl in my immediate present is stirring now, a soft moan emanates from her chest. I'm not sure but I think she actually wants me to, you know, go down on her. *She's too beautiful. Way too beautiful for you. You don't deserve her. You'd be taking advantage of her. You must have drugged her!* No! *Date raper!* What? *You'll only make the whole experience ugly.* I'm sorry! *Don't drag her down with you!* I would never. *Just let her be.*

The chorus of voices, too numerous to name, bark their various forms of expurgation from inside my head. Sometimes I wish they'd just shut up. The overwhelming consensus of voices, however, have effectively brought me to my senses. Quietly, I slide out from between her sweet legs, put on my now wrinkled suit and collect my things, putting them into my canvas bag. I slide my Palm Pilot into the pocket I've made in the bag to keep it safe. I slip out the door as she yawns and stretches, cat-like, rolling over onto her stomach. I close the door gently behind me and slip out a rear entrance. Sad as it may be, sometimes it's best to walk away and not look back. Still, I wish I could have brought myself to touch her, at least once.

Chapter 3
10:13 a.m.

NOW I SIT, ALONE, IN THE cool refuge of this windowless restaurant; I think it's called something like, "Lucky Cheng's." What's a Chinese restaurant doing in the French Quarter? I try to regroup, as I pick at the plate of rice I'd ordered reluctantly. That's OK, it was the coffee I was after.

On the way here, I noticed the whole French Quarter had been transformed since the chaos of last night. It's become a ghost town, as if there never were a Mardi Gras. It reminds me of an episode of *Star Trek* where an entire planet of people goes crazy at the midnight sounding of a bell; they lose all inhibitions, raping and destroying one another. At noon, a second bell rings and they become as docile as sheep. It all happens at the bidding of a computer, named Landru. Perhaps Mardi Gras is at the arbitrary whim of an unseen computer as well. Maybe this whole thing is the "will of Landru." Maybe our entire existence is really only the clever computer projection of some sadistic, spoiled brat sitting at his console, somewhere in the cosmos. *You watch too much TV.* I know.

Down the street the girl in white is probably sipping her own morning coffee. She's gone now and I am alone again—back on task. The low rumblings from the air conditioner motor under the floor console me. "Hey, can I get some coffee over here?" I mutter to the waitress. She looks like a Tonkanese Madam.

The ventilation ducts have become hairy with the black soot which inevitably attaches itself to grease. The ancient brown drippings on the beige tiled walls make a lovely abstraction. I raise my hands, forming my thumbs and forefingers into a square to create the four corners of a picture frame. I can see a number of excellent designs but I quickly lose interest and drop my hands. I hate it when restaurants refuse to clean. Do they really think it would ruin the ambiance if they tidied up once in a while? Or are they just lazy? The place is an incubator for rats and roaches, for Christ's sake.

I make a clean spot on the table and pull open my Palm Pilot; I continue in my journal. My stylus moves with a practiced agility and speed:

> *I feel closer to the other side of my longing now, as if I'm emerging on the far side of a very long tunnel. Maybe that's why they call it longing. I used to fantasize about a magic pill I could take that would make everything all right. When Prozac came out I was all over it. I talked a psychiatrist into writing me a prescription. He charged me for a full session, even though it only took five minutes. The drug produced an overwhelming feeling of well-being, deep in my solar plexus. That, along with a complete lack of interest in anything sexy, including sex, was more than I could take. I quickly returned to the periodic whining to friends that kept my demons at bay in the days before pharmacologists hijacked the field of psychiatry. For all my dire introspection, I've never really been*

able to say whether I'm basically an optimist or a pessimist. I've always had a keen sense of the ideal. One thing I know for sure: it is transforming to have identified that missing piece; to be on a mission, to be certain, for once, that I am in the right.

Aye, there's the rub. I'm about to take another man's life. This murder, however, has a moral imperative. This creep deserves his fate.

Believe me, I once thought there was another way. Or should I say, in retrospect, if things had gone differently–if I were made differently, if certain people had not done what they did, or failed to do what they should have done, if certain information didn't present itself, if we lived in a world where truth existed in some absolute form, then this wouldn't have been my only clear action. But on the deepest level, after all the layers of truth are peeled away, does anyone really have a choice? Can anyone choose their destiny once it has been so clearly revealed?

Even if we were able to convince ourselves that we could change our fate with action, wouldn't we only be expressing the inevitable? We cannot win a fight against God–if there is a God. We can only plod along, trying to convince ourselves we have any control at all. Control is the ultimate delusion.

No. Clearly, there is no choice. There is a man in New Orleans who will finally pay the price for what he did to me so many years ago.

I lift the cold cup and saucer to my lips hoping the coffee might cause a slight downward adjustment to my equilibrium, which has been disturbed by these thoughts. I wish I could silence the chattering in my mind. *That's the coffee cup rattling against the saucer, you idiot.*

Now as I sit alone, staring down at the marvelous designs made by the remaining food I've left on my plate, I consider the wisdom of my fortune cookie. "It is sometimes better to travel hopefully than to arrive." I crumple it up and flick it onto my plate, along with the black clump of rice I've so skillfully rolled into a ball between my fingers. God knows what I just ate. Where's the waitress?

Wait a minute. Here's a fragment. I recall something more about last night. I remember talking to the girl in white, talking her ear off, in fact. We ended up alone above that antique shop. We could hear the muffled crowd pounding outside. She must have had a key. She must be living in that second-floor warehouse, among all those antiques. She wanted to know about me. I remember telling her all about myself. I was a wellspring, blabbing away. She was asking questions as fast as I could answer them. "What made you leave New York City? Why do you draw so much? What brought you to New Orleans? What do you think about when you draw? What were you like as a child?" I'm such a sucker for the attentions of a pretty girl. And she was definitely attentive. She seemed sincerely interested in me. What if I said too much? *It wouldn't be the first time.* Usually, when I try too hard to open my heart, I end up opening my mouth instead.

Bloody Mary emerges from the kitchen and picks up my masterpiece from the table, scraping the brilliant abstract from my plate into a bin containing a variety of other food remains. "While you're at it, would it be too much trouble to bring me some more coffee?" I ask politely. Does she even understand me? She hasn't spoken a word or even looked at me the whole time I've been here. Ever since I got off the plane, I've been feeling like a bit player in a Tennessee Williams play.

Did I slip up and tell the girl in white the reason for my trip? Did I, in the heat of my reveling, reveal his name? I remember rambling about my childhood. I always do. Everyone does. That's harmless enough. For most people, childhood is insulated by an unspoken statute of limitations and remains separate and distinct from who they are as adults. *They're called boundaries, asshole, and you don't have them!* See, that's a perfect example of what I'm talking about!

Wait a minute. The girl asked me what *made* me leave New York. Not "why did you leave" but what "made you leave." Why did she say, "made"? What did I say to make her use that word? *Come on, you were driving the conversation. Did you betray the mission?* I don't remember. *Think, man!* Did I slip and tell her what *made* me come here?

There was something familiar about her. What was it? What does she know about me? Could my sketches have somehow revealed my plans? Did I make a mark, a sweep, a scribble that expressed too clear a purpose? Did I leave behind a line that might implicate me later?

My sketchbook! I unzip my bag and look. Oh my God. It's gone! Where did I leave it? *You're such an idiot! You left it in her apartment!* Oh shit. *You've got to get it back!*

I suddenly feel woozy, like the bottom has dropped out of my circulatory system. I need some water. "Hello! Can I get some water here?" I shout into the back room, through the once brightly colored fabric hanging over the door. Where did she go? Where is everybody? *You stupid idiot! You've blown the whole thing!* What time is it? My Palm says 11:40, New York time. Have I gained an hour or lost it? Why am I the only one eating here? The goddamn place is deserted. Where are all the people from last night? Where's my cover of chaos? *Something's not right about this! You've screwed the whole thing up!*

I'm startled by the piercing sound of my chair screeching against the floor as I thrust myself up from the table. I throw down a twenty; that should cover the bill. I click off my Palm Pilot, stuff it into its place in my bag, lunge open the door and leave.

The piercing New Orleans sun glares down on me like an interrogator's light. I run down the center of a narrow street. My eyes adjust to the colors in the shadows, which begin now to emerge from the blinding whiteness. Everything is clean and bright, like a movie set.

The streets are beginning to fill with people again. That's a good sign. But now there is a slow motion to the throng. Everyone seems to be nursing either a hangover or a spiritual awakening.

A rotund hot dog vendor lumbers across my path pushing his hot dog shaped cart in front of me. Why is he wearing a hunting hat in this heat? What a kook! As I swerve to avoid him I nearly run into two oddly shaped women who are meandering off the steps of a large cathedral. Make that one oddly shaped woman and one cross-dresser, both smeared with ashes across their foreheads. Oh, that's right. Today is Ash Wednesday.

The only thing moving as fast as me are the little black children mindlessly dancing with bottle caps nailed to their sneakers, klickety-klacking, hustling for pennies on the sidewalk. I slow down, closer to the pace of the crowd. I bend over to catch my breath.

Everything's all right, now, everything's fine, sings the voice of Mary Magdalene from *Jesus Christ Superstar*. Where'd that come from? The voice is soothing, a welcome departure from the norm. It's amazing how certain tunes suddenly pop into my head. Inevitably, they always contain some message that drives me nuts until I figure it out.

Okay, wait. I left no identification in my sketchbook. No names. No addresses. No words. Nothing. Just my lines—my drawings. Nothing admissible in a court of law. No one cares why I'm here. No one knows my name and even if they did, what have I actually done? Nothing. Have I broken any laws? No. I've left no trail. Just the sketchbook. And the girl. She's the only one I've spoken to down here. *You'll have to kill her too.* No! She seemed harmless enough. Who was she? *You better find out before you take another step.* If there is a God I can only pray I didn't tell her anything important. *Goddamn it, why did you drink so much? What an asshole!* I know. I know.

The trouble with me is I worry too much. That's because I think too much; at least I think I think too much. I'm not sure. I'll think about it tomorrow, just like Scarlet O'Hara.

On the other hand, I don't go chasing all over the fucking globe to hunt down and murder evil specters from my past every day either. So I guess I should expect to be a little nervous, under the circumstances.

I wonder if the girl in white has looked at my sketchbook. She must have. Did I leave it there or did she steal it? *Don't you dare try to pass this off on to her.* I'm sorry. Either way, I've got to get it back. I can feel my testicles undulate slowly at the possibility of seeing her again.

Is that actually a pay phone? It's camouflaged very well. It looks more like an old-fashioned utility box. The receiver smells like a woman's perfume—very sweet—Youth Dew, I think. Once again, I feel my testicles undulate in my pants as I dial the phone. *What a pervert!*

"PJ?...Yeah, it's me. Yes, I made it down... What do you mean you didn't think I'd come? Well, I'm here. I got in last night...it's a long story... No, I didn't have a chance to check my e-mail... No, I don't have a wireless modem or a cell phone... I don't like them...because the government is able to trace my whereabouts... Yeah, just like Osama Bin Laden... No, I'm not a terrorist... I'm sorry you were worried... No, I'm all right. I'm fine... I'm sorry... It's good to hear your voice too. Listen, I'm going to try and find your place, I'm going to head uptown... Take the what? The streetcar? Named Desire?... Okay, the St. Charles... Alright, I'll meet you there as soon as I can."

I hang up. The sound of PJ's voice, deep and dark, has a calming effect on me. Come to think of it this is the first time I have actually heard her voice. As I mentioned, she and I have only spoken over the Internet, Instant Messaging and e-mailing across the ether. We've gotten to know each other pretty well, considering we've never actually met.

It occurred to me that I might need a safe place to lie low after executing my sinister plan in New Orleans. I managed to get myself invited to her home during my visit. I can only imagine what this poor woman will do when I show up, covered in blood. Of course, she knows nothing about my mission. Funny, she seemed almost surprised I actually made it down. Under the circumstances I probably shouldn't have taken her up on her offer but try finding a place to stay in New Orleans during Mardi Gras. I'd heard about people selling old mattresses for hundreds of dollars just for something to sleep on.

As PJ herself said in so many of our e-mails back and forth, "there are no accidents." I'm beginning to believe it. I feel for the first time in my life that everything is happening as it is meant to happen. I'm beginning to sense a line connecting all the seemingly arbitrary events of my past, present and future.

What a magnificent place this is. The sun seems to turn everything to gold. There would be so much to paint here, if that's why I'd come. Ever since I was a child I've always looked at the world around me and imagined the corners of a picture frame closing in around the scenes that move me. I crop them into magic rectangles, squinting my eyes, until they become a fully composed, fully realized painting, even if only for a second. In that instant, I can see the gesture of each stroke. Each line, edge and color comes together, taunting me with their variety and balance. Then as quickly as it appears, my window to the world fades into the dim recesses of my memory and another emerges to take its place. Sometimes it makes me dizzy. But it always makes me sad to lose these pretty pictures, each one a potentially compelling work of art. I guess that's why I still sketch so much. In a way, putting pen to paper confirms for me that what I see is really there.

I have been an artist all my life. But now, with the exception of my sketchbooks, which I almost always discard or give away—*or lose, you idiot*—I have completely weaned myself of any artistic designs—pardon the pun. It's such a release, to be free of all those lofty aspirations. I have found again and again that there is no one more likeable than a *former* artist. After all, being an artist carries with it such an awesome obligation and responsibility. And yet art itself is merely a byproduct; the excrement of one's unending search for truth.

I guess that's why society treats its artists like second-class citizens, relegated to the margins. As a society we have almost convinced ourselves that we don't really need art. It's true. Art serves no practical function. If it doesn't match the sofa then it has no business being in the house. If it doesn't provide more than a 7% return on the dollar it's a waste of our hard earned money. It's a common misconception that money can buy culture. It can't. Artistic expression requires a tremendous force of will, both to accomplish and to appreciate.

So I finally asked myself, "why bother? What have my talents gotten me?" Sure, I've made some money with my talent, quite a bit really. Now, I've achieved a kind of cultural equilibrium: I owe nothing to society and society owes me nothing in return. The more I think about it, the more I'm almost glad my sketchbook's gone. It just puts me one step closer to letting go of the past completely.

At least I was spared the greatest humiliation an artist can endure: never finding a way to sell his work. Like my father, I'd come to believe the sale of an artwork was the consummation of the creative process. It's heartbreaking to consider poor Van Gogh never had that experience while he was alive. *Do you think that makes you better than him?* Better? No. But at least I can say I enjoyed financial success as a professional artist.

Now that I have simplified my life, stripped it down to its essentials, the whole thing begins to make perfect sense: it's all been just a game, a warmup for the real thing. This is the first time in my life I've actually had something real to do.

THE FISHFLY

My epiphany was long in coming, however. My destiny only revealed itself to me about two months ago. It was back in New York City.

Chapter 4
Dr. Gusto Fernandez

"WHY DO YOU WORK SO MANY hours?" asked Andy. He and I were among the growing army of artist/actor/musician temps lubricating the financial machine on Wall Street. This was the first, and hopefully last, "real" job I would ever have. I was a word processor at Morgan Stanley, working at an hourly rate for brokers and their insipid secretaries. I was just beginning to enjoy the Zen-like monotony of prettying up their mergers and acquisitions, IPO's and disposition documents.

"You get paid the same whether you work this hard or not," he interrupted again, trying to make conversation. But I remained silent, staring blankly at my terminal, clicking purposefully at the keys.

Thanks to places like Morgan Stanley and Goldman Sachs, artists, actors and musicians need no longer starve as they wait to be "discovered." The downside is that temp money is like a narcotic that robs the artist want-to-be's of their creative aspirations, which, come to think of it, is probably the best thing for them. I was working alongside "artists" who had been temping for as long as twenty years. For me it was perfect. I had very little responsibility and I was able to rack up quite a pile of cash in a relatively short period of time. The hardest part of the job was being condescended to by gum-slapping secretary/supervisors from New Jersey with acrylic nails and decidedly limited world views.

Finally he snapped, "Hey, man, take a break already!" I stopped and eyed him coldly. Andy was an unpleasant cross between a displaced California beach bum and a pushy New Yorker. We had struck up a friendship of sorts. "Lighten up, man. You were typing about 150 words a minute. You trying to break a record?" I broke into a slight smile, which only encouraged him. He pushed on. "I don't understand you, man. You've been putting in, what, fifty, sixty hours a week?"

"65," I said, wishing I could return fully to what I was doing.

"Yeah, well, I don't know why you don't go back to painting portraits, now that you're back on your feet again. From what you said you were getting for them, man, you should go back to it. What are you hanging around here for?" He was right: I made more on one portrait than I could make here in six months.

I turned back to my terminal, but he kept going. "You don't need to be here, man. What are you even doing working in a hellhole like this, man?"

"Look, 'man,'" I said, finally, "why don't you go back to California, 'man.' Can't you see I'm busy, 'man'?"

"Where's your copy? What the hell are you working on?" he demanded as he leaned in over my shoulder to see the e-mail I had been composing. "I can't believe you. It's him again, isn't it? I mean, what do you want with this guy?" he pressed, seeing the name of the recipient. He spun my chair around to face him. I was silent, continuing to stare in the direction of my monitor.

Andy was the one who had helped me locate my nemesis, a certain Dr. Gusto Fernandez. Pronounced like Mucho *Gusto*. Andy was handy with the Internet. I hadn't told him the reason I wanted to find him. "Why are you still e-mailing this—" suddenly hushing his voice into a whisper, "degenerate asshole. He's a fucking pedophile, for God's sake? What could you possibly want with this freak? You can't do anything about him over the Internet."

Finally, I stopped and looked him squarely in the eye and darted, "Stay out of my business, Andy. What I do with my downtime is my concern, so fuck off." I resumed typing my e-mail. Eventually, Andy wandered away. *What a jerk!* He's not a jerk. *Not him, you!* True friends, those actually concerned about your well-being, are hard to find, especially in New York City.

When I first started working there he might have expected a moment or two of witty, even lighthearted banter from me. But that was before I stumbled onto Gusto.

It's providence that I should now be so close to seeing him face to face again, after so many years. I didn't plan for it to happen. It just did.

During my abundant downtime at Morgan Stanley, I'd usually "surf" the Internet, searching for something. I don't know what. I found myself exploring the electronic ether the way I once scanned the newspaper classifieds or the Yellow Pages. I was sure I would recognize whatever I was looking for when I saw it. Something in the vast unknown had always been calling to me.

My compulsive searching had been a long-standing addiction. I tried to pass it off as simple curiosity but I later came to realize my endless hunting came from a deep-seated emptiness in my life. I spent years looking through books, surveying various landscapes and scanning people's faces, looking for something, an answer to that burning question: "Why me?" I could have easily spent the rest of my life aimlessly hoping for meaning to magically reveal itself to me. Then one day I actually found what I'd been looking for all along. It was on a particularly slow day in data resources, while I was casually surfing the World Wide Web. While mindlessly browsing a secure University of Minnesota Medical Resource Directory, I inadvertently found myself connected to an Internet search engine from the rain forests of Brazil. *Gusto was from Brazil.* A dim light went on in my head.

While on that site I discovered a link to another search engine. It was a database of Brazilian medical research facilities. Because I was using my corporate ID and because my inquiry originated from Morgan Stanley, I was able to gain access to this information. I had created a secured, anonymous login and password with Andy's help.

My heart began beating faster as I continued to narrow my search. I swear it was just a lark. I hadn't seriously tried to find him in thirty years. But after numerous half-hearted searches I finally had a list of three Dr. Gusto Fernandezes, all of whom had conducted research in Brazil. Two of these researchers were radiologists. Gusto was a radiologist. Each name on the list had a user e-mail address along with various nicknames to protect their identity. But because I had found these names through Morgan Stanley's "secured" database, I had clearance to obtain a wealth of personal and professional information about them.

One of the two radiologists had a series of curious nicknames: "Dr. Nice," "NamblaMan," and "Rainfo." It was almost too perfect a match. I needed a way to determine for sure if this was actually my man.

Andy helped me gain access to his personal profile, which provided information such as his home address and special interests. It also contained reports on his various research projects. He seemed to be quite active in experimental studies using natural compounds from the rain forests in the treatment of AIDS. It said he was also an adjunct professor at the Tulane

Medical School, in New Orleans. I even managed to find his curriculum vitae. That's when I saw the entry: *1973-75, Radiology Internship—Children's Hospital, Detroit, Michigan.* There was no question about it. It was him.

From the moment I found Gusto I've been overwhelmed with a sense of purpose. It was the first time in my life I knew exactly what to do. I'd found my calling.

I could have simply e-mailed him, or even called him using the phone number in his personal profile. I chose rather to use caution. Protected by the anonymity of my Morgan Stanley account, I discovered several other search engines. I had to find a backdoor into his world. I discovered an environmental activist news group that dealt with research in the rain forests of Brazil. I read each subject with mounting excitement. There were a number of ardent participants. I found the heading: "Looking for like-minded friends."

I scanned each entry for his various nicknames and eventually found an open letter authored by "Dr. Nice," entitled, "Need a Friend." He had composed a personal statement, which read, "Looking for thought-provoking conversation with real people interested in getting down to the truth. Age no barrier." It turns out he had placed numerous personal ads in a variety of social activist forums. I could only imagine the lively correspondences "Dr. Nice" had been carrying on with young boys from all over the world.

The beginnings of several such relationships, displayed in public forums, were scattered throughout the domain. He would correspond in public for a while, then the letters would suddenly stop, to be continued in private Instant Messages and encrypted e-mails, to which I could not gain access. It was overwhelming. I felt a combination of elation, dread and revulsion.

I decided to start with a public reply to "Dr. Nice." I created a fictitious personal profile and introduced myself as a 14-year-old boy in need of a friend. I called myself Flyboy.

"Dear Dr. Nice," I wrote, "are you a real doctor? You must be so busy." I created an entire persona and played it to the hilt. I came from a wealthy family, living in Akron, Ohio. I had everything I could possibly want but somehow I still felt empty. I was often allowed to travel alone and dreamed of one day falling in love and running away with someone special. Soon, Dr. Nice had Flyboy eating from the palm of his hand. Actually, it was quite the opposite. I was laying the bait and luring him in for the kill.

After that, we began a fury of private e-mails back and forth, each one more intimate than the last. Like his other on-line friends, we moved to chatting and Instant Messaging back and forth. We talked about everything. He gave me advice on made-up girlfriends, living life to the fullest and not accepting mediocrity. It was just like old times.

I'd hate to imagine what would have happened if my supervisors, the dim-witted secretaries, found out I was digging up old skeletons on company time. That would have been very unlikely. Whenever a supervisor came along I just clicked onto another screen. I really had no idea what they were paying me for.

The whole scheme was so devious; pretending to be a young boy, tracking down and drawing this slime bag into my trap, plotting, planning, having such a malevolent goal. But I felt so grounded, so driven, as if I were on a divine mission.

Eventually, Gusto convinced my alter ego, Flyboy, to meet him in New Orleans where he would "liberate me from my fears, once and for all." After a convincing period of coyness I'd told him I would really like to meet him. He'd pushed the same old buttons he'd pushed so long ago, sprinkling words like love, integrity and honesty into conversations about rising above the moral codes of others, how the sexual norms in Brazil differ from those in the States and what it means to be a fully self-actualized human being. It was like reliving my past, only this time, I was in control.

Chapter 5
Me

THANKS TO ALL THOSE EXTRA HOURS temping, I was able to clear up all my debts. I'd closed all my bank accounts and gotten rid of everything I didn't need, even my most treasured possessions. I gave the inventory of my paintings and supplies to the local thrift shop and my clarinet to the little boy on the fourth floor of my apartment building. I threw away the letters and the boxes of stuff I'd hauled around for years. All I really needed was my Palm Pilot, a few changes of clothes and enough cash to finance my get away and live for about a year or two abroad.

I feel so much lighter now. I remember a line from a sermon I heard long ago: "The gates of heaven are narrow indeed." I wonder if I could make it through the heavenly gates via the World Wide Web.

I've completely given myself over to the cause. "It is the cause, it is the cause," wept Othello. Oh yes, that reminds me. I also used to be an actor. I trained extensively in New York

City. I approached acting with the same uncompromising zeal with which I pursued all my artistic interests. I used to be considered a "Renaissance man," a man of the arts. *You're so goddamn cocky.* Absolutely! There's a direct relationship between a low self-esteem and extreme arrogance. Yes, I know all about my game. I'm self-aware enough to know I'm an incurable egotist.

Let's see, what else can I brag about, while I'm at it? I'm a singer, I played clarinet very well until I gave it away last week and, as we've established, I'm pretty good with a line. After years of reflection and intermittent therapy, I realized I'd been attempting to prove my worth to others by calling attention to myself through my talents and force of will. I've grabbed a lot of accolades. But never enough. I should have known I was in trouble when I won class clown *and* earned a 4.0 GPA in ninth grade. Ironically, it is my insatiable need for approval that has kept me prisoner all these years. Now I realize it was all an elaborate attempt to compensate for the unconditional approval I never received as a child.

In recent years I've lived as anonymously as possible. I've become a man of few words. In short, I have evolved into "no one" of the Cyclops' curse. Like Odysseus—and Captain Kirk—I have wandered through the wilderness in search of the great unknown. The flashes of brilliance, the glib arrogance and anger of my twenties gave way to the more trail-blazing existence of my thirties. Now, in my forties, I understand a little better the delusion I'd been living. It's scary to think how far I've come. Here I am, deep in the bowels of the Mississippi delta, about to come face to face with my destiny.

One casualty of my youthful arrogance was my familial attachments. I changed my name legally when I was 24. I refused to ride on my father's considerable reputation as one of the most highly regarded portrait artists in the Midwest. Ironically, it was he who suggested I change my name. "I don't want people to confuse your work with mine." God forbid. He once told me Detroit wasn't "big enough for the both of us," adding, "there are only so many slices of the pizza to go around." I took this as ostracism, plain and simple.

That's when I moved to New York City. I wanted to start over, completely. In retrospect, I'm pretty sure his "pizza" comment was intended as a perfunctory admonishment. Either way, with a single-page form at City Hall, I transformed myself from Donald Minello, son of the great Anthony Minello, into Donald Michael Spinelli, son of no one.

I think the real reason I changed my name was because, deep down, I was literally trying to become someone else, someone, perhaps, with a more accepting father. I wanted to leave my sorry past behind. Becoming someone else was the next best thing to finding true self-acceptance. Maybe someday, I'll have the real thing.

The name change turned out to be very good for me, professionally that is. I figured while I was reinventing myself I might as well make up a few other things. I made a few minor improvements to my portfolio. I took Kurt Vonnegut to heart when he said, "we are what we pretend to be." I painted portraits of princesses, presidents and personalities. I created sumptuous paintings of Mother Theresa, Oprah Winfrey, Ronald Reagan and William Shatner, the eminent nobility of our time. People naturally assumed these luminaries had commissioned me; I didn't correct them. It wasn't long before people like these actually were commissioning me. I found out that real talent in combination with artful manipulation is an excellent recipe for success.

I soared ahead. I established an international reputation from my studio in New York City. In time, my father came to envy me, though he never let on. It mostly came out in conversations he'd had with others that made their way back to me.

He blamed my mother for convincing him to leave New York City in order to be near her family. Then, after the divorce, with his children "tying him down," he was never quite able to "get back into the game."

Then about five years ago, my father had a debilitating stroke, for which I've blamed myself. I was there when it happened. He's a complete vegetable now. I still find it incredibly painful to imagine him that way. He was always such a man of action. After his attack, I just couldn't bring myself to paint anymore. My family tried to assure me it wasn't my fault, that I couldn't have *caused* him to have a stroke. But I knew I had. I'm arrogant enough to blame myself for everything that's wrong in the world. I would have made an excellent Jew, Catholic or existentialist.

Soon after the stroke, I left Detroit and never went back. Eventually, I stopped answering phone calls from my family. They were my last connection to a past I no longer wanted to remember, even though I knew, no matter how hard I tried, I could never forget. Visions of my crazy older brother William, tickling me until I couldn't breathe or my boisterous sister Stacey's cackling laugh continue to both haunt and amuse me. I can still see my mother, who even after she quit smoking twenty years ago, was still sucking on straws the last time I saw her.

Chapter 6
Rufus Hastings

IT WAS A COUPLE OF YEARS after my name change that I met Rufus Hastings. He was quite taken with one of my portraits, which moved, along with its subject, from New York City to Natchez, Mississippi. While visiting from Savannah, Rufus told my patron, "I just *have* to have this artist do my portrait."

So Rufus flew me down to Savannah, where I created what was to become one of my most commanding portraits. Rufus met me at the airport in a white Rolls Royce accompanied by an African-American chauffeur and whisked me away to his three-story town house in the historic district. It was that first impression I would paint. He wore a white cotton suit with a red bow tie. He was the most charismatic and elegant individual I had ever met. He was tall and slender with snow-white hair. Although his family had made their fortune in cotton, Rufus capitalized on his keen sense of good taste by becoming one of the South's preeminent antique dealers and interior designers. He was something of an impresario.

Apparently, he had chosen to come out of the closet sometime in his forties. He was rumored to have gotten into trouble with the law over an incident with a young boy, but I found that difficult to believe. He seemed to transcend labels of any kind. Rufus easily wandered in or out of the closet as it suited him. He was completely at home in his skin and had the uncanny ability to make everyone he met feel incredibly special. It was hard not to admire him and the world he had built around himself. There did seem to be an awful lot of paintings depicting children, however.

"Just because you're born a Yankee doesn't mean you have to die one," he once said to me as an aside. It was just one of the many asides he made during his multifarious champagne toasts. He was famous for producing elaborate soirees, nearly every evening, for a careful mixture of friends and potential clients. He astonished his guests with lavish multi-course gourmet dinners, served by young Nubian menservants, dressed in pretty silk cocktail dresses, who came when he rang his tiny dinner bell. "Don't mind us, Donatello, we do things a little differently down here."

I spent an extraordinary week with him in his three-story townhouse in historic Savannah, while working on his portrait. I had never seen such an amazing conglomeration of fine art and antiques in one place, except in a museum. He was the very image of a blue-blooded southern aristocrat. As flamboyant as he was, he never exhibited the slightest pretense about his opulent lifestyle. For him it was all done in pursuit of pure aesthetic, sensual gratification.

His estate was a wonderful play land for him and his friends. It was replete with gilded furniture, extravagant silver services, and massive fresh flower arrangements in bounteous porcelain vases, approaching, but never crossing the line into vulgarity. Paintings by Peter Paul Rubens hung over plush, fabric covered walls, which were appointed with luscious draperies, pouring without apology onto the floor. He balanced his excesses with an ingenuous warmth and grace. He had a natural gift for making everyone in his home forget about the formality and grandeur all around them, while at the same time inviting them to revel in the beauty and sensual detail with every sweep of his hand.

My painting sessions with Rufus were magical experiences indeed. His body cut an amazing line through the air. His fine, sculptured features caught the light to form endlessly fascinating abstract shapes for me to paint. I wielded an impressive array of brushes, pulling lights into darks with an ease that comes only with inspiration. I managed to capture a certain mischievous, almost sinister quality, just beneath the smile. I don't know where it came from but it seemed to suit him.

On the third day of my trip a sweet little girl came to visit. Alicia was her name. She was Rufus' daughter from an early marriage. She was about eight or nine years old. I remember thinking at the time how young she was to be dealing with some of the unusual lifestyle choices being paraded openly in that home. Alicia wandered aimlessly through the house, entertaining herself with imaginary friends. No one paid much attention to her and she didn't seem to mind, doing quite well in her own little world.

"So you're the artist who's painting my father's portrait," she declared in a lilting Georgine drawl.

"Yes, I am."

"It's coming along very well. I saw it," she said, matter-of-factly.

"Thank you," I responded, with a humble bow of my head.

"I'm going to run away with an artist someday." She was easily the most precocious, charming little girl I'd ever met. She was one of those rare human beings who had a way of bringing me out of myself by the sheer simplicity and genuineness of her being.

"Why settle for running away with an artist when you could become one yourself?"

"I wouldn't want to spoil the magic of painting by learning how the trick is done."

"You'd rather believe in the magic?"

"Yes, I would."

"Yeah, me too."

Nonetheless, I remember talking her into a number of mini art lessons during my stay at the Hastings home. But it was she who was doing the teaching. I had almost forgotten the magic of creation, the poetry of self-expression. We talked about everything. She prodded me with soul-feeding questions I'd long since stopped asking myself: "What do you see when you smell a flower? What do you feel when you pull red paint into blue? What is the sound in your head when you're drawing? Would you draw me if I asked or would you charge me a small fortune?" I drew her with pleasure, no charge.

In the evening of that third day, Rufus summoned me to his room. It was near his bedtime when I entered his boudoir. He was naked except for his silk bikini underwear. I remember feeling uncomfortable but not threatened.

"Should I come back later," I wavered.

"No, come sit by me," he said as he gingerly tapped his bed cover. I took a few steps toward him and stood by his chiffonnier.

He reached across his down bedspread and put his reading glasses into the drawer of his nightstand. His quick eye caught me noticing the gun in the drawer. "It's a sad commentary on the world, isn't it?" he said with a sigh. "I always keep a gun in my nightstand. I find I just can't sleep without it. There are people in this world who would stop at nothing to steal the things I keep in this house. It's a shame, isn't it?"

"Yes, it is. Sometimes I think it's a miracle we survive the madness in the world," I said. "Would you use it if you had to?"

"Probably not," he said simply. "I'm sure it will only lead to tragedy someday. But somehow it provides me peace of mind, so I keep it around." He closed the drawer, using this point as a segue into a charming attempt to seduce me. Somehow it didn't offend me. Even though he was my patron I felt no pressure to succumb to his advances. By this time in my life, I had become pretty adept at deflecting the flirtations of men, who for some reason tended to find me attractive. I was no longer the slightest bit curious or unclear about my sexual persuasion. In a way it's a shame. My heterosexual inclinations have in effect cut my pool of potential lovers in half.

He made one harmless request, however. "I just…I just want to kiss your eyes. They're beautiful and I want to be able to feel what they see." He kissed my eyes delicately. I let him know I appreciated his kind attentions and excused myself. He didn't push the issue, for which I was grateful. He seemed certain that eventually I would come around to preferring the love of a man, as he had, later on in life. After what happened with Gusto when I was fourteen, I can't say this statement didn't make me a little uncomfortable. But I sensed, even then, there was a deeper purpose for our friendship. So I let it go.

I hadn't thought about Rufus in years. I had no reason to be in touch with him, outside of the true pleasure of his company. I no longer needed him as a patron, having left the profession, as it were. But then I heard he was now living in New Orleans. Guess how I found that out? Two weeks ago, after much prodding from Gusto, my Flyboy persona had told Gusto that he was thinking about getting away from his folks and visiting him in New Orleans at Mardi Gras, after one of his regular symposiums at the Tulane Medical School. I ventured to ask where he would be staying. Imagine my amazement when he said he would be the guest of an old friend of his, named Rufus Hastings.

At first I couldn't believe the incredible coincidence. But

then, when I thought about it a little more I could see the connection. Since they seemed to share a common interest in young boys, it only made sense they might run in similar circles. Who knows, they may be part of some strange underground vortex of pedophilia. Judging from the stuff I'd read on-line from Gusto, anything was possible.

    Either way, it made my job much easier. I found Rufus using a simple on-line people search. I called him a few days later and told him I might be coming to New Orleans for a visit. He was delighted at the prospect of seeing me again and invited me to Ash Wednesday dinner. He wasn't able to offer me a place to stay this time around, however. He was "full up" with house guests.

    I told him that was fine, which it was, as I had made other arrangements anyway, which I had, with PJ.

Chapter 7
My Father

I WANDER INTO THE HEART OF the French Quarter. So this is Jackson Square. I'd read about it on-line when I was getting ready for my trip. It's a little more manicured than I'd imagined. The sketch artists are out in droves, tossing off one generic sugarcoated pile of crap after another, selling their souls at $25 a pop, the price of a really bad blow job. That's got to be tough, sitting out in this sun all day. I'm grateful to have been spared this particular form of humiliation.

Hmm, what's this stool doing here in the middle of all this heavy "commerce"? What the hell, it's something to sit on. It's hot and my feet are rebelling.

Thanks to my father, I never had to peddle my talent. His professional expertise set me years ahead. It was because of his mentoring that I was able to pull off my successes as a portrait artist. Not that his training didn't have its costs. I had to put up with the indignity of his denigration. He used to love telling people, "I taught Donny everything he knows," adding with an elbow to my shoulder and a wink, "but not everything *I* know." He truly was a masterful painter and had the gift for translating his formidable skills into a language I could understand. I was devout in my study of painting. At every stage in my career, however, he always made it clear to me he didn't think I would ever live up to his high standards and expectations. Perhaps he believed an ever rising bar would motivate me to transcend the limitations of my talent. Maybe he felt threatened. Who knows?

I remember bringing him a portrait I'd been working on. It wasn't finished but it was one of which I was particularly proud. He was still in the hospital, just after the stroke. He was barely able to speak.

I was hoping my presence wouldn't upset him any further. I thought my bringing him a painting might take his mind off his deteriorating health. My plan seemed to work. When I brought it into his room he perked up and struggled to speak. I moved my ear closer to his mouth. Barely audible, yet clear as a bell, he said, "You've over modeled. If I've told you once, I've told you a thousand times, 'When in the shadow, to get more form, go darker.'"

Those were the last words anyone ever heard him utter. He winced in pain, then fell asleep. I sat there, holding his hands for what felt like hours. He was suddenly so vulnerable, so helpless, like a baby.

I felt a wave of guilt. Was I gloating? Was his demise in some sick way a personal triumph? Or, were his final words a final humiliating blow? After all, he was right; the painting did need an awful lot of work. I never finished it. In fact, it was the last time I ever painted.

I left town soon after my visit to the hospital. I'd heard he'd had a series of strokes which eventually left him in a vegetative state. I don't even know if he's still alive.

I was never able to tell him how sorry I was about what happened between us. I didn't want to agitate him or make him feel any worse than I already had. "There are certain things you just don't talk about." That's what he used to tell me. I guess this was one of those things.

Early on, my father used to joke that all I had to do was add a zero to the end of my price to get his. He was actually very comfortable treating his art as a commodity. I wasn't, at first. But eventually I caught on. Early on I was an idealist. I was a very self-righteous artist, which is the worst kind. My father was self-righteous, don't get me wrong. But he was fortunate not to be self-righteous about *being* an artist, which meant he was well liked by everyone, except other artists. This was particularly true of those artists who believed selling art meant selling out. "I don't give a rat's ass what these people think. What do those goof balls know about making a living? They don't have to support a family with their art. They get paid to teach others how *not* to sell their work." My father made no bones about it: he was after commissions not awards or fellowships.

His artistic talent, along with a generous helping of neurotic predispositions were his genetic endowment to his children, although I'm the only one who actually went into painting. I'm the baby of the family. You can tell by the conciliatory way I stick my chin out, trying to be noticed but really asking for a punch in the jaw.

My parents decided to get divorced when I was nine months old. I was one of those babies conceived with the intention of injecting new life into a failing marriage. My mother's biggest disappointment as a parent was that she couldn't keep her children in a drawer and take them out to play whenever she wanted. In fact, her last day in our home was my earliest and most vivid memory. Somehow, this memory reached beyond the veil of repression.

I was in my crib, watching my mother pace back and forth as I quietly lay there. Then, the next thing I knew she was gone. It's amazing how clearly I can see the sky-blue walls and the emptiness of that room, yet I can barely remember what I did last night. I can still feel the breathy summer stillness and the shit falling out of my diapers. I was trying to stuff it all back inside with my hands and feet. I remember feeling profoundly dirty. I wondered, was this what my life was to be about, wallowing in shit, forever? The more I tried to make it go away the more of a mess I made. I remember the moment when I gave up trying to make it go away. I started smearing the shit all over the wall in great big circles. I remember making the decision to accept the wretched creature I was becoming. There was a serenity to it. How could I have known I was an early pioneer of the fecal art movement?

"You remember that day?" my father would gasp, twenty-five years later.

"Yes," I answered simply. "I remember lying there for a long time covered in my own shit."

"You were there for over six hours," my father blurted. "You wiped your shit all over the wall."

"Oh, you didn't like my mural?" I looked at him, half smiling. He didn't appreciate the irony; he rarely did.

"When I came home and discovered you," he continued, "I knew right away what had happened. Your mother went to some kind of a political rally. She couldn't wait for the sitter to get there so—"

"She must have thought the housekeeper would show up," I interrupted, instinctively wanting to defend her.

"Well the housekeeper *didn't* show up, Goddammit." He looked at me quizzically. "I can't believe you remember that day."

I turned and stared straight ahead, overwhelmed by the many answers flooding in, answers to questions I had never been able to put into words.

"That was the straw that broke the mammal's back," he went on with what sounded like wounded pride. "She was gone for good after that." He paused, long and hard. Then he looked into my eyes and furrowed his brow. His upper lip curled hideously and his eyes grew dark with a hatred that froze the moment forever in my memory. "Your mother…" He didn't have to finish the sentence.

After having completed the painful task of giving me life—I was a breech birth—my mother "cut her losses," as my father put it, and got out while she still could. In all fairness to her, he wasn't the easiest man to live with. He wouldn't let her work or go to school. In his mind, her only job was to rear his children and clean the house, in accordance with the old Italian tradition. This was during the emergence of feminism; then she joined N.O.W. The timing of this convergence was devastating to their fragile marriage. She claimed, years later, it was his tyranny that drove her into the comforting arms of Phil Nader down the street. My father insisted it was those bra burning fanatics she was seeing.

After a nasty divorce my father was given full custody of me and my two older siblings—unheard of in 1961. We saw my mom every other weekend after that. Raising three children single-handedly while pursuing the precarious career of an artist was no easy feat for my father. In fact, it was nothing short of miraculous. But, living with all that guilt heaped on her over the years was no easy feat for my mother, either.

Back then, there was no such thing as a "no fault" divorce; blame was everything. Frankly, I didn't care whose fault it was. Their breakup resulted in my having to spend the greater part of my childhood without a mother. I don't recommend it. My friends' moms and teachers filled in whenever possible. For instance, Russ Raining's mom made bologna sandwiches just the way I liked them. But at the end of the day my father was stuck being both mom and dad to me.

It was written in a newspaper article once that I was my father's clone, a "chimp off the old block," as he used to refer to me. It's true. I wanted only to be like my papa; he had the answers to any question I had as a kid. Unfortunately, he continued to have them past the age when children need to find out some of the answers for themselves.

When I was eight I painted a pretty strong portrait of him, signing my name, "Minello, Jr." He pointed out that because our first names weren't the same I "couldn't technically get away with using the 'Jr.' bit," in my signature. Obediently, I painted it out, nodding my head, my mouth hanging open, as it often did when I wanted to disappear into myself.

This had become my automatic response whenever I was presented with information I was already supposed to know, which was quite often. What is it about the obvious that I've always found so difficult to grasp? I feel so out of the loop; whenever I'm confronted I just go limp. Scientists have recently discovered that our reactions to stress are at least 30% genetic. Maybe I can blame that on my father too.

"Stand up straight and close your goddamn mouth," my father would bark. "You look like some kind of a mongoloid or something." He wouldn't tolerate self-pity in any form, not even for a second. He had a very clear image of himself as the consummate "good guy," the great avenger of bullies, enthusiastically offering himself to me as a model for human virtue. "I was the guy wearing the white hat," he boasted. "No son of mine is gonna walk out of this house looking like a *retard*," he declared, mimicking my unattractive posture. "After all, look at me," as he put it so often, "I pulled myself up by my jock strap and raised three kids without anyone's help."

While his efforts to support three children were valiant, I couldn't help wondering about all those other "guys" who might happen to be wearing different colored hats than he. Were these guys somehow *not* good? My father was never plagued by such questions. To him hats were strictly black and white. He thought of himself as the kind of a man who would "draw a line in the sand, daring anyone to step on it."

My father was a relativist only in his paintings, which were filled with subtlety, grace and variety. After his divorce in 1961 he enrolled in the Dale Carnegie course in assertiveness, which, as he put it, got him to "wake up and smell the caffeine." His moral absolutism, loosely based on Darwinian codes and garbled Benjamin Franklin quotes, seemed arbitrary and random to me, but he was bigger and far more verbally agile than I, so he won every argument. I was the product of social relativism which grew out of Einstein's theory of relativity. For me, everything was relative. Unlike Einstein, however, I accepted being wrong as a way of life. I learned very early; my own judgement was not to be trusted.

Once, when I was five, a family friend watched as my father, who had volunteered his services as a scenic painter for the local community theater, asked me to stir a bucket, into which he had poured two different colored paints. When he returned in a few minutes and saw the paints were not mixed, he thundered, "I told you to stir this paint. When I tell you to stir, I expect you to do as you're told."

The friend, who had observed the whole affair, interrupted quietly, "You know, Tony, one of the colors you put in that bucket is oil based and the other is water."

Furious, my father barked back at the man, "You've got a lot of nerve. Who do you think you are, interfering in my family business?" He went back to belittling me until I said I was sorry, which I was. I was always sorry. I had the self-esteem of a sloth.

Sleeping was my only sanctuary, which really aggravated my father. That's probably why I enjoyed it so much. For him it was simple: "Early to bed, early to rise makes a man stealthy, wealthy and wise." He never really seemed interested in what I might actually be depressed about.

A few years later, when I was eleven, I stumbled onto an interesting solution to my problem with over-sleeping in the morning. I would leave an exposed electric cord plugged in next to my bed. After I turned off the alarm I would simply touch the wire and zap! The little jolt was all I needed to get myself "up and at 'em." I no longer had to hear those words from my father every morning. My invention meant an end to his bellowing threats and castigations down the stairs to rouse me. All it took was one tap of the wire and I was up those stairs faster than a wayward glance.

By this time I had inherited my brother William's macabre basement bedroom. Weighing down the end of a pull-switch light was the femur of a chicken drumstick. The window wells were covered with a thick black cloth, which blocked all unwanted light from the outside world. A makeshift occult shrine stood ominously in the corner, complete with an empty cologne bottle in the shape of a Buddha. It looked like the ghastly lair of a serial killer. I got to sleep in his room whenever they checked him into the nut house. Otherwise, I slept in a bed behind a curtain on the other side of our dingy basement.

William didn't adjust well to our parents' divorce. He would occasionally punch holes in the walls or hurl rocks through our picture window to underscore his arguments with my father, which could never be won with words. He blamed my father for driving my mother away. He and my father were constantly making scenes, screaming so loudly the entire neighborhood would close their windows and doors. My brother had no inhibitions about expressing his extreme disapproval of the way things were being run in our home. To say it was an unstructured environment would be an understatement. But burning down our garage was a little more than even my father could deal with. William denied the whole thing, blaming it instead on three black boys with white shirts or three white boys with black shirts. He couldn't remember which. Behaviors like these resulted in several periods of residency (translate: incarceration) at the Lafayette Psychiatric Clinic.

Don't get me wrong, I enjoyed sleeping in his room. Secretly, I always wished I could stand up to my father the way he did. But after several days in "the quiet room" and a little shock treatment, William's anger would dissipate long enough for him to return home. Eventually, when he became a born-again Christian it went away entirely. "In the beginning, there was repression."

Fortunately, my electric wake-up method was discontinued before it was too late. One morning, my sixth grade teacher, Mrs. Williams, interrupted her regularly scheduled lesson and brought me up to the front of the class. "Donny," she prodded, "would you please tell everyone how you've managed your exemplary improvement in attendance? Have you finally discovered that discipline is its own reward?"

I hesitated for a moment, not sure if I should reveal my *shocking* wake-up method before getting it patented. But, not yet having developed the ability to fabricate a lie on the spot, I found myself describing my new low-tech, electric wake-up technique in intricate detail.

She gasped, "You do *what?*" From her tone and the buggy-ness of her eyes, the obvious danger in which I had been placing myself became immediately clear.

I persisted in my justification anyway. "How else do you think I could ever get here on time? I mean, it's not like any of us actually look forward to coming to this crummy school." The class found this very funny. She didn't.

She put the class captain in charge and escorted me to Mr. Ballard's office. He was a large, always well-dressed man who loved being *The Principal*, though I suspect he really aspired to being the superintendent, perhaps even making a run for the state senate, someday.

Whatever the offense, Mr. Ballard's punishment was always the same. He would jab the amputated stub of his middle finger into my shoulder. I couldn't help but wonder if this might be painful for him. I suppose he intentionally played on this uncertainty in order to amplify the guilty feelings of those he punished. It was really quite brilliant. The image of his poor, emasculated finger smashing against my hard collarbone was far more painful than any actual pain he might be inflicting on me.

By the time I reached his office I had already assumed my gaping-mouth, mongoloidial slump. He emphasized the key words of his lecture with the repeated jabs of his pitiful, stub-of-a-finger: "I've *called* your *dad*, son. I *think* you're going to *have* to find *another* way of getting yourself to *school on time*."

When I got home my father had just finished re-attaching what used to be my handi-dandi-live-wire-wake-up device to the toaster, which of course had been without a cord since I'd borrowed it for the live-wire-wake-up device. My punishment for being so industrious? He would no longer participate in the morning car pool with my friends' parents. Mr. Ballard was right: I *would* indeed have to find another way to get myself to *school on time*.

By the time I was fourteen I had learned to appreciate my father's immense artistic prowess but still hadn't gotten my head around his intense volatility and arbitrary moral code. Like most fourteen-year-olds, I wanted nothing to do with my father.

Fourteen was a pivotal year for me. I had spent my entire childhood up to that point in the rather pleasant suburban community of St. Clair Shores, hugging the shores of Lake Saint Clair, northeast of Detroit. All the houses in my subdivision looked pretty much alike, variations on a three-bedroom ranch house.

This was 1974, a year that was to become a record summer for fishflies, which are sometimes referred to as shadflies, Canadian soldiers, June bugs or mayflies. The fishflies were just beginning to make their annual appearance, loitering on window screens and dancing around the streetlights. In later years they had nearly become an endangered species, with all the pollution in the lakes. Fortunately, fishflies have more recently made a dramatic comeback, a sign of improving environmental conditions. I'm glad, as I've always felt an unusual affinity with the little creatures. Loathed by most for their smell and overwhelming numbers, they were like little shimmering beings to me. They seemed so patient and kind, not skittish and excitable like other bugs. I had a strange communion with them; they seemed so content on my finger.

On hot summer days like these most neighborhood boys my age were out hunting for pollywogs or playing kickball in the streets until the streetlights came on. I remember one typically hot, humid day in June when I got inspired to paint a knock-off of David's, "Napoleon on Horseback." I was working in acrylics, on canvas, down in the cool clamminess of my basement where the humidity slowed the drying of the paint long enough for me to work with it a little.

Even so, I found myself struggling. I couldn't get the new paint I was applying to blend with the earlier layers. In mounting desperation, I began adding more and more water, hoping its cleansing properties might somehow make everything okay. But the water only made it worse. Napoleon was dripping off his horse, off my canvas, right onto the tray of my easel and there was nothing I could do to stop him. I began to panic.

Then, at the last possible moment, when I was about to lose forever what was to have been my all-time masterpiece, I caved in. With rueful reluctance, I called upstairs to my father, "Pa, would you help me, please. I'm having trouble with my painting." Down the stairs from his studio he rushed to my easel. It had been over a year since I'd last asked for his advice. He was very "old school" in his approach to teaching. But this time he seemed unusually happy, even eager to interrupt his own work for me. Maybe he was hoping for another chance to bond creatively with his son.

He glanced at the dripping mess and without hesitation, hocked up an enormous loogie and gobbed it onto my masterpiece. Inside, I repressed a sustained, high-pitched scream, which shot directly up my spine and lodged into my brain stem. Outwardly, however, I fell into the same, automatic, semi-mongoloid posture.

I couldn't believe it—not even *he* was capable of such an abominable crime against his own child. Oblivious to my agony, he grabbed the dripping brush from my hand. "If I've told you once, I've told you a hundred times," he lectured, "there's the right way to do something and there's the easy way." I watched in horror and awe as he rubbed the gooey mucus into the paint, working it in. "There it is…that's got it."

The extra viscosity of his spit rescued my Napoleon from oblivion. "Now *that's* the right way," he declared as he flicked my brush masterfully on the canvas, easing my painting back into submission like a horse whisperer. He handed the brush back to me and darted away. He hopped gleefully up the stairs to the kitchen where he turned his attention to preparing a delicious lentil soup, which was his specialty.

Faintly I could hear him singing "Invictus," which I believe is the Latin root for the word, vindictive. I'm not sure. He sang it often, though. He had a way of turning his head to the right and tightening his throat to make his voice sound more "operatic," at least to his ear. He sang, "I am the master of my ship. You have to stand up and fight for what is right," something like that. He often boasted they were the only lyrics he never forgot. Him and Timothy McVeigh.

All other songs he sang in gibberish Italian. It didn't matter what song it was. He always made up just the right Italian-*sounding* lyric to sell it. He would close his eyes and grab his heart, bellowing quasi recitatives that went something like, "Noche, pia noche, *pistaccio*." He was a ham all right. Actually, he was well known for his Italian gibberish AND his bad memory, just two more of the charming eccentricities for which he was so well liked.

Oh yes, the painting. I finished it. It came out pretty well. In fact, I sold it to Dr. Amberg down the street for five dollars. I'd asked for eight. I gave my father a dollar as a consulting fee. By fourteen, I was well on the way to acquiring my father's gift for commerce as well as his artistic methods and proclivities.

"Okay, my friend, I'm finished," says a deep voice with a thick Creole accent, snapping me out of my nostalgic reverie.

"Excuse me," I say to the source of the voice, an extremely thin black man with a thick white beard and sunken eyes.

"I'm finished," he repeats, holding a dim likeness of my face up for me to see. "That'll be twenty-five bucks."

"I'm afraid there's been a mistake," I say.

"There's no mistake," he insists, a little intimidatingly, holding his open palm out to me. "You've been sittin' in my chair an' I been drawing you. Now you pay me. That's the way it work."

"No, I'm sorry. I was just resting here a minute—"

"You was resting in my chair."

"I didn't realize—"

"Ignorance of the law is nine tenths of the law."

"I think you mean 'possession is nine tenths of the law.'"

"What?"

"Either way, I'm not sure how that applies in this case. Look, I'm sorry about the misunderstanding."

"You mean you don't want to pay me, mista?" he says, holding the sketch up again for me to examine.

I open my mouth to tell him, *I wouldn't pay two bits for a piece of shit like that; I'm certainly not going to pay five dollars above the going rate.*

But instead I point to what clearly should have been the shadow side of my face in his sketch and say, "You see this? You've over modeled. When in the shadow, to get more form go darker."

As he withdraws the sketch, scrutinizing what he has just drawn, I pull out a $20 bill, drop it into his box of student grade pastels and walk away. The nerve of that asshole!

Chapter 8
12:24 p.m.

I SLIP INTO THE ALLEY NEXT to the St. Louis Cathedral where I remove my Palm Pilot from its padded case inside my leather briefcase.
 I no longer write words on paper. That's so last century. Besides, paper is reserved for drawings. I don't remember the last time I wrote a word on paper. What would be the point? It's all in here, in my tiny Palm: everyone's address I've ever known, every thought I've ever had. It also contains all the letters, back and forth, between Gusto and me—even our earliest "chats" between Brazil and New York. The only way anyone can reach me now is over e-mail and all my e-mail identities are aliases. I keep very little information in my head. My Palm Pilot compensates for my feeble internal hard drive. My bad memory is just one more genetic gift from my father for which I've had to acquire an appreciation.
 I look up Rufus Hastings' store address. It's 1:30 p.m., New York time. I wonder how you change the time on this thing. I

can go to the ends of the earth via the World Wide Web but I can't figure out how to change a goddamned clock to Central Standard!

Hmm. This looks like the same row of shops the girl in white took to me last night. That's kind of weird.

I need to find a bathroom, straighten up a little, get my bearings. I walk into a loud bar on Chartres. I head toward the bathroom.

"Not so fast, son," says a brick of a man with tiny, inbred eyes. "You can't use the john unless you're a customer." His eyes never leave the skinny, naked woman, center stage, who's in the act of rubbing her crotch all over a fire pole.

What exactly does he mean? *Does he actually expect me to pay money to have sex with this pathetic woman? What kind of a town is this?* "Excuse me. I don't understand..."

"You gotta buy a drink, son." *God, you are so naive! Stupid's more the word!* I buy a Coke. It calms my stomach a little. I leave the glass on top of the urinal, after I've peed in it for spite.

That's better. I'm back on track. Now, it's on to Rufus' store. I told him I'd stop by around one o'clock. I'm either half an hour late or half an hour early—damn time zones are so confusing. Is Central Time earlier or later? Let's see, the sun goes—

Hold on; this can't be right. I think this is the same antique shop I walked through last night. It is! *Wait a second. Hold on a minute! Don't go in there.* The girl in white is right upstairs. Who is she for God's sake? *What's she doing above Rufus' shop? What if she turns out to be Rufus' daughter, you jerk.* No, she can't be. Maybe she's a renter. *You fucked Rufus' daughter.* I can't believe it. *You've blown the whole plan.* Wait a minute! How could she have found me in all that confusion? The age is right, but...no, it's impossible. *Yeah, why would she be sleeping with you?*

No. Stop. This is no time for self-loathing. I have to find out what's going on here before I go any further. This is too much of a coincidence. *Don't you get it? It's a setup, asshole.* Wait a minute. I've got to figure this out. Okay: Rufus is the only person I told I was coming, besides PJ. He's the only person who knew I was arriving on Mardi Gras day from the airport. That's all I told him. *You gave him the arrival information, didn't you?* Yes, I think so. *Obviously, he told his daughter.* Yes, he might have. *You idiot! What should I do? Abort! Abort! You've blown your cover.* No wait. Calm down.

That's Rufus inside, giving instructions to a couple of his pretty, young stock boys. Nothing's changed.

Holy shit, I think he sees me! I'm committed. I can't walk away *now. Walk away, now! Don't go in.* I have to go in; he sees me. I'll have to figure this out later. *This is never going to work. Look what you've gotten yourself into.* I am in the hands of fate now.

He emerges from the front entrance of his shop, spinning flamboyantly toward me on the ball of his left foot. "Why, you *did* make it down here, you rascal, you." I smile widely into his chest as he hugs me to his heart. It's impossible not to be completely swept away by his charisma. "You haven't changed a bit, boy. You're still as handsome as the devil."

"Oh, I've aged a little," I add sheepishly.

"Oh my, my, oh MY! My, look at those beautiful eyes," he says lyrically, firmly placing his hands on my chin and peering right past my eyes, straight into my soul. I wonder what he sees. "You're coming to supper tonight." He's not asking. He's simply stating a fact. As he speaks he holds my head in place with one hand and hypnotically strokes my hair with the other. He has me locked in the tractor beam of his charm. "Now listen. Lemme tell ya. Now…now…I have some people I want you to meet tonight who might be interested in having a portrait done." *No, don't let him press the money button!* "Dante Simms is going to tickle the ivories and I want you to sing and play your clarinet. You did bring your ax?"

"Oh, no…" I say, doing my best to feign disappointment, "I didn't bring it down with me. I'm sorry, Rufus."

"You remember Dante from Savanna?"

"Oh…sure…"

"I remember the way you two carried on together."

"We played well together, too," I add, anticipating what will undoubtedly be a witty series of double entendres for which he is so famous. *You think you're so clever but you're not!* True, I find it usually works better for me just to allow innuendo to go over my head.

"Oh, you old devil. You so bad. You are the worst. Boy!" He mocks southern Ebonics to perfection. "You know he lives in New Orleans now, right around the corner, in the Marigny."

"Oh really, who?"

"Dante."

"Oh really, where?" My nervous questions have broken his rhythm. I take a deep breath and try to recover the moment, "Maybe he and I could go over some songs before tonight; that is, if you'd like me to sing, Rufus? I'm not in good voice, but—"

Rufus' graceful fingers release my head and reach for a yellow sticky. "I think that is a stupendous idea." He writes Dante Simms's address on the corner of a gilded, eighteenth century, inlaid mahogany desk. I notice it has a $60,000 price tag on it. Somehow, a yellow sticky just doesn't belong on such an object. "Now, you know there are some people I want you to meet." I don't dare tell him I've stopped doing portraits. He hands me the sticky as the bells to his shop door jingle.

In walks an older version of my nemesis, Dr. Gusto Fernandez.

IT'S HIM—THIS IS REAL! My heart flushes its entire contents downwards to replenish the cells, which have just died deep in my abdomen. *Don't move. Breathe, you idiot—you'll give yourself away!* My whole body is shutting down, cell by cell, one organ after another.

"Well, well, well, speak of the devil," Rufus gushes. "Now, now, now, this is the worst rascal there ever was. Lemme tell you, this boy is sooo bad—well now, lemme tell you, Donny, he's so bad he'd make Sammy slap his mammy." They laugh heartily as they embrace warmly. "I want you to meet my dear friend. Donatello Michelangelo Spinelli, this is Dr. Gusto Fernandez, the greatest physician in Brazil. Donatello is that famous portrait artist from New York City I was telling you about."

Everything's in slow motion now. Rufus has done well, obfuscating my past for me. *But what did he mean by, "telling you about"?* What if Gusto makes the connection? Does he recognize me? Can he tell who I really am?

Gusto reaches out his hand, which I shake firmly. *This is it. Don't blow it*, says the voice of frenzy from my shoulder. *Do only what is appropriate and logical for the moment.* Can he hear my heart, which has sputtered into beating again with a defibrillating jolt, bashing at my chest? I fight to erect a wall between our gaze, slowly and inconspicuously taking very slow, deep breaths. *Don't you dare show any sign of recognition. Close your mouth and stand up straight, for God's sakes!*

I am looking directly into the eyes of my past, present and future. Both horror and astonishment are suspended in the air between us. Can he feel the energy moving through our hands? *Cut the shit. This isn't an episode of* Star Trek. *You're gonna blow it!* Does he recognize me through my impression of an easygoing smile? I want to jump out of my body. *Jump! Do it!* Maybe I have. I feel like I could explode at any moment.

"A pleasure to make your acquaintance," some part of me says, feigning what I hope is an appropriate degree of sincerity. I think I just lost several million brain cells.

"Have we met before?" he asks, searching my eyes for a clue. He finds none *as if people really can read minds!* The world has gone brown as I struggle to process what is happening.

Indeed we had met 25 years before. Gusto was my sister Stacey's first love. He was a promising young doctor, a resident on the Radiology staff at Children's Hospital in Detroit, one of the most highly respected children's hospitals in the country. A true ladies' man, Gusto had all the charm of Zorro and all the looks. He had a cultivated, soft Brazilian accent. He was a most desirable bachelor by any standard—certainly by Stacey's. She had long ago lowered her criteria for a mate; she was ready to settle for anyone who paid her the slightest bit of attention. For her, Gusto was beyond her wildest expectations.

"You're going out with a doctor," pressed my father, dissembling an obligatory disdain, even though he was undeniably impressed.

"And why shouldn't I go out with a doctor?" she *valley-girled* back, defensively. "He's gorgeous! And he treats me like a queen."

"We treat you like a queen," interrupted my brother, William, his eyes widening to an insane grimace. "Here, Queenie. Here, Queenie," he howled, calling her like a dog. Stacey was on her way out the door for her first date with Gusto. She had stopped back home to pick up the orange dress she had worn for prom the year before. She was living in a dormitory now. It was the beginning of her first year of nursing school at Grace Hospital, in the Detroit Medical Center.

William continued with his taunting, "Sit, Queenie! Roll over, Queenie!" He derived true pleasure from tormenting my sister and me. He was particularly cruel to her but he was quite adept at finding and pushing everyone's hot buttons.

None of this was going to upset Stacey. She had found a doctor who was more than willing to treat her like his little Barbie. Finally, she got to be the wide-eyed nursing student she always imagined, the envy of her entire class. She was the only one of her friends who had landed a date with an attractive and distinguished doctor. She had found her Ken.

She was more than grateful. Apparently, Gusto had more respect for her chastity than she did. As far as anyone knew he never made a move on her, never tried to pinch open her bra with one hand. No awkward groping or pressure of any kind. Amazingly, he seemed to enjoy "spending quality time" with her.

In fact, Gusto was soon spending quality time with our entire family. He said he missed his own family very much. That was no problem. Ours was more than happy to fill in. He often let me tag along when he and Stacey went out on their "dates."

He intuitively knew how to make everyone in my family feel incredibly special. William liked him because he laughed at his jokes. Gusto certainly knew my father's hot buttons. He claimed he personally knew each member of the portrait selection committee at Children's Hospital. They were in the process of choosing the artist to paint the outgoing chairman of the board. This commission would have been a "real medal in his cap," indeed. My father was doing everything he could to help Gusto feel right at home.

"You've all been so very kind to me," he said during one of our many family outings. "I feel a love for you as if you were my own family," he declared, handing Stacey and me our ice-cream cones at the Dairy Treat near my junior high school.

"Let me get this one," my father interjected, a little too late. Gusto had already paid while my father was parking the car.

Gusto continued his adulation of Stacey and me, oblivious to my father, "I hope you'll forgive my honesty. I believe in saying what is in my heart."

"No, don't be silly. There's nothing to forgive. Jeez, it's so sweet, Gusto." Stacey and I gushed, falling all over ourselves to make him feel accepted and comfortable.

"What'd I miss?" interjected my father, trying in vain to be included in the moment.

"We love you too," she blurted as I nodded my head in agreement. "Yes, we love you too," I added, a beat later than was appropriate. No one had ever spoken to us like this before. I couldn't remember the last time anyone in our family had said, "I love you."

I take a deep breath before my legs give out. "No, I can't imagine that we've met," I lie with a polite detachment, moving my eyes back to Rufus and releasing my hand from Gusto's firm grip.

"You look a little warm, Mr. Donatello," Rufus says, noticing my condition, despite my best efforts to conceal it. "Would you like a glass of champagne…freshen up a bit? You're not used to the heat down here, are you, boy?"

"No, I'm not. But I'm fine. Actually, I have to go and…rehearse with Dante for tonight." *Just get out of here!* "If you wouldn't mind…excusing me, I'd probably better…go take care of…that…right now." *Breathe, you idiot!*

"I'd be very happy to drive you," Gusto offers graciously. He hasn't lost a bit of his old charm. I think I'm going to be sick. *Oh, you're sick alright! You're definitely not up to this. You'll never be able to pull this off! You better get the hell out of here while you still can.* No, I'm on a mission.

"That is very kind of you but I think I can find my way," I mutter. "Will we see you later tonight?"

"Well, I'm…" Gusto fumbles this time. There! It's in his eyes. He clearly has not made the connection to our common past. There is a delightfully awkward pause.

Rufus rescues the moment. "Well, of course you will. Donatello's talking about dinner tonight. You'll be there, won't you, Gusto?"

"Oh, of course. I wouldn't miss it for the world."

"Good. That's all taken care of, Mr. Donatello. We'll see you at six thirty."

I make my exit. I'm pretty sure they're not onto me. *Don't be so damn cocky about it. You almost blew it.*

I find my way back to the same pay phone as before, this time with a different aroma. I don't recognize it. First I call PJ to tell her I'm running a bit late. Then I call Dante Simms who, not surprisingly, invites me for an impromptu rehearsal at his apartment in the Marigny District, just outside the French Quarter.

Fifteen seconds after ringing his bell I hear the clank of a key whistling by my head and hitting the pavement. I look up, scanning for the origin of the toss. A curtain is flailing out a window on a fourth-floor balcony, dripping with overgrown plants, engorged with what must be a constant supply of loving care. I use the key to let myself in and climb the winding staircase to an open door on the fourth floor. Chopin beckons me into Dante Simms' apartment. Boy, is he good. "Dante," I call out, following the sound to its source. He continues to play as he speaks, a skill I always admired in my brother, who played piano quite well, but more as a way to get under people's skin than from any impulse to make music.

"So, what's got you crawling back down this way, Mr. Don?" Before I have a chance to answer he rattles, "Did you bring your ax with you? I remember our little duo. I had big plans for us, you know. We were going to gig around, remember? Rufus bring you down?" Again, no chance to respond. He speaks extremely rapidly in one continuous stream of consciousness. "I knew he wouldn't let you slip away for good. He likes you, you know. We all like you. *Liked* you. Well I guess I still do, even though you went away. Rufus is Catholic now; did you know that? Or at least he pretends to be. He made the switch over from *Christian Scientists* when he moved us all here from Savannah. No one knows about it, not down here, anyway, so don't tell him I told you. He didn't go through catechism, you know. Didn't need to. He already knew the ropes. He's a wonder. You *do* know he got run out of Arkansas for molesting a young boy?"

I think Dante's playing the Polonaise in A flat major, Opus 53. "That wasn't very smart of him," he continues, without missing a beat. "He's usually very smart about getting what he wants. He's quite a wonder. Did I already say that? Well, it's true, he is. He tried to get me to join. I'm talking about NAMBLA, not the church. You can feel that man-boy-love energy just oozing out of him. I'd join the Catholic Church before I'd ever join that mess. It's just not my thing. I'm not into children. I think that's sick, don't you? I like my men. Not old men, mind you. But children? There's a whole chapter down here, of NAMBLA, that is. North American Man Boy Love Association. Don't tell him I told you so, though. He'd frown on my telling you anything of the sort. So you didn't hear it from me. Because, he's a good man, all in all."

Dante is either on drugs or should be. It's amazing how he is able to play Chopin and be such an amazing cad, all at the same time. Finally, there is a pause in his monologue.

"I'm here to go over a song or two for tonight," I lie. I've already got much more than I came for. But like the magic-music-making machine that he is, he segues into the introduction to one of the grand old songs of the South, one I sang so many years ago: "Old Black Joe."

After we run through two or three additional songs, I make a quick exit. I hate rehearsing.

Chapter 9
PJ

I FIND MY WAY TO THE St. Charles trolley station on Canal and head uptown to check in with PJ. I want to make sure I have a place to crash after I've eliminated Gusto. Hopefully PJ won't ask any questions. She'll respect my privacy. She's always been so understanding in our e-mails.

I take this opportunity to review more of what I've written recently on my Palm Pilot:

> It seems so clear to me now, all that remains of the past is our memory of it. We are constantly reinventing and improving our memories, adapting them to our current needs. The people who have had an impact on our lives speak to us through our thoughts. Trouble is, what they say does not remain fixed. Sometimes they sing their gentle messages into my ears, while other times they scream incessantly like vultures, tearing at the flesh of my scalp, trying to get at the soft spongy wetness of my brain. These ever-evolving voices are

the music of life, like the tunes that suddenly pop into my head for no apparent reason. But I know there are no accidents. The past is an invention of the present.

What is this crap? I don't know, but at least I'm calmer now. I almost lost it back there with Gusto and Rufus. That won't happen again. I think I'm starting to get the hang of his cloak and dagger game. I hate to admit it but I'm almost beginning to enjoy the adventure in which I find myself—all this plotting and manipulation. Being "authentic" was never as much fun. What's the harm in a little game-playing now and then? At least I know what I want. The rest will take care of itself.

I remember a few years ago, when Andy and I decided to con our way to the top of the Chrysler Building. First, we had to convince the security guards we belonged in the building. We made up fake employee IDs and walked right in. Of course, this was before 9/11. We were so nonchalant about it. But what a payoff. We climbed all the way to the top, to the stainless steel skewer. Andy was too scared to climb the scaffolding to the very highest point. But I hadn't come all that way to chicken out. I climbed right past the cathedral windows, open to the warm June sky. There I was, alone at the top, on a four foot square platform, overlooking the entire city. From up there I remembered my father's words. "Son, when I look out over the world I see a vast faceless throng of people. They're all the same, except for one, who stands above the fray. I want that person to be you." I could have so easily stepped off the platform and slid down the glistening stainless steel spire of the Chrysler Building, to my death.

I continue writing into my Palm Pilot:

Until this moment I had always been one of those sad saps who was stuck in the rut of trying to be honest. But I think I was really just hiding behind the idea of being "authentic" or "real." It was just a way of keeping myself locked into the same tired paradigms. Our subjective, distorted view of truth is what passes for reality. We elect presidents who brag about their honesty, their unwavering constancy, even though we all know we'd be better served by someone who had the courage to change course when they were proven wrong. Perhaps we could all learn a thing or two from our sociopathic friends, like Gusto and Rufus, the ones for whom people like me are always picking up the pieces. We are the saps who listen attentively as they toss around words like "honesty" and "integrity," as if saying them were the same as doing them. Why is it I'm always falling prey to people who know how to get away with anything?

Who says we must cede to people like O.J. Simpson, Michael Jackson, Kobe Bryant or even—God forbid—Gusto Fernandez, the right to transcend the social order? Don't I have the right, the responsibility even, to choose my own fate? As Gusto himself once wrote in one of his many political diatribes to me, "justice is because it just is. Laws are made to be broken."

Oh Christ, this is my stop! When did it start to rain? When I left the quarter it was a bright sunny day. Where did the clouds come from? Man, there's some wacky weather down here. Quickly, I tuck the Palm Pilot back into my bag and follow my directions to PJ's, using my canvas bag as an umbrella.

I stand in front of what must have once been a charming shotgun home. It's very quiet except for the white sound of rain and the incessant nagging of a single buzzard in the towering sycamore tree above my head. I look up and see only leaves.

"Hey," I yell upward, into the thick canopy. The buzzard stops as if somehow to acknowledge the inappropriateness of his behavior.

I look back down. A striking woman in her fifties has appeared at the door. Her eyebrows are raised at the center. Her lower lip is pushed forward into a permanent pout.

"I'm sorry. I was talking to the buzzard."

"Well then you must be Dr. Doolittle," the woman says sarcastically, her face relaxing back to a more attractive neutral.

I double-check the address. This is the place. "Are you PJ?" She nods her head. "And who are you?"

"It's Paul. I'm Paul." Okay, I lied to her about my name. I wasn't kidding when I said I'd given up being honest. Besides, this is a secret mission.

"You're a little late, but no worse for the wear," she lilts in a sarcastic Arkansas drawl. We stand there for a good long moment, nodding our heads, sizing each other up.

"Sorry about that," I say, dripping, sheepishly on her porch, trying to defuse the awkwardness of the moment. "Can I come in?" She looks coolly at me for another moment, then swings open her door.

"You're a little wet. I'll get something for you to put on." She turns and disappears into one of the rear rooms of her long, narrow flat. I stand dripping on the worn-out square of linoleum just inside her front door. She's older than the picture she e-mailed me, but 'no worse for the wear.' She's very generously equipped. Actually, she looks pretty much like I'd imagined her. Her blondish silver hair sways in response to the rhythmical bouncing of her surprisingly voluptuous body. She looks a little like Marilyn Monroe might have looked if she had lived another twenty years.

She told me over e-mail that she was the top majorette in her high school before dropping out to marry the man who would father her two children. She claimed Bill Clinton asked her out.

THE FISHFLY

That should have been a warning sign for something. But what?

I recognize the telltale upturn of her Barbie-like nose. I doubt if she used the same surgeon as my sister but the look is unmistakable. Stacey has the same profile. There is a whole subculture of women who dye their hair blond and get their noses bobbed to look like Barbie. I've seen them on several daytime talk shows so it must be wide spread.

As a child Stacey constantly played with her collection of Ken and Barbie dolls. Great marketers had lighted the fire but little girls like Stacey and PJ made it burn. Ken and Barbie were the model of platonic romance. Stacey molded her life after these genital-less dolls of her youth. They were her only refuge during the arduous breakdown of our parents' marriage.

Over the years, Stacey—and I strongly suspect, PJ—made all the appropriate changes to their bodies. Poor Stacey has lost all feeling in her lips and chin, the unfortunate result of an operation to bring her mandible forward so it might line up better with her Barbie nose. She'd always struggled with her weight. My father once sent her to Florida to stay with his sisters for a couple months. He gave her a bottle of diet pills, telling her how beautiful she would look when she returned at the end of the summer.

When my mother left, Stacey became the only female in the home, taking on the burdens of motherhood with none of its rewards. She did the best she could, but her resentment slipped out on occasion, especially when William and I refused to obey her maternal commands. Once, she chased me around the house with a lit cigarette for refusing to wash the bathroom sink. Tormenting Stacey was how William and I displaced the frustration of living in our chaotic household.

When I was about five my mother returned home to take a second crack at motherhood. My father refused to actually remarry her until she passed his strict measure of marital rectitude. She didn't. And when she left again it sent us all into a deep depression. My response was to crawl under a chair in kindergarten, refusing to come out. Mrs. Fickner pleaded with me in her thick German accent.

"Please, Donald, von't you come out unt play vith the rest of ze boys unt girls?"

"Go away, I hate you!" I wanted to die.

"I vill send you down to Mr. Ballard," she threatened. Rather than lose face in front of her class, she wisely chose to summon Stacey over the PA system from her fifth grade classroom. Stacey charged into the room and with a firm yank, at once reasserted her motherly authority upon me. Her inner child died the day my mother left the second time.

I raise my hands reflexively, to protect myself from a swatch of silk hurling toward me. "Go ahead and put this robe on," comes PJ's voice. "You can take a bath if you want. Use the towel closest to the tub in the bathroom."

"Thanks," I say as I tiptoe across her carpet, doing my best to drip as little as possible. I close the bathroom door behind me and take off my poor suit.

"I'm doing a wash," PJ calls through the door. "Do you need anything done?" I reach down into my bag.

"Yeah, thanks." I unpack and hand her my laundry, consisting of three pairs of underwear, three pairs of sox, two shirts and a pair of comfortable pants. I hold onto my black pants, black shirt, black ski mask. She doesn't need to wash any of those. I haven't worn them yet.

"What I really need is to get this suit pressed for tonight."

"Why? What's happening tonight?" I hear the crank, click and splash of a washer. I sit down on the toilet behind the safety of the closed door.

"I've been invited to a dinner party," I yell over the sound of the washer.

"Well I guess you don't waste any time, do you?" What does she mean by that? It's a little early in our "relationship" for her to be getting possessive. *What makes you think she cares what you think?* I'm pretty sure I had told her over e-mail that I had planned to attend a dinner party tonight.

I reach over and start the bath water running. We raise our voices one more notch, to be heard over the washer and the bathtub.

"There's a dry cleaners around the corner. I'll drop it off for you, if you want."

"That would be great, thanks," I reply. She reaches around the door, groping for the suit, which I place in her waiting hand.

"I'm so used to talking to you over e-mail," she shouts. "It's kind of a trip to see you face to face, if you know what I mean."

"Yes," I call out as I sit back down on the pot, clutching a towel securely.

"You get used to the clarity of it, you know," she ventures. "No bodies to distract you. Just two minds connecting in the ether, your imagination filling in all the sights, sounds and smells."

"I hope I haven't disappointed you," I goad.

"No, not at all. I think you're very attractive."

"Thanks." I shit as stealthily as possible. "You too. I mean, you know, I think you're very attractive too."

"Thanks. You know it's funny, I feel more comfortable talking to you from out here," she says.

"Yeah, I know. I feel the same way."

This is the first time I ever wooed a woman while taking a dump.

"It's a little unusual but it works for me." Hmm, does this mean I'm supposed to stay in here until she feels comfortable?

Every surface in her bathroom is cluttered with a large assortment of makeup, skin creams and a complete line of Opium perfume products. "You're the first person I ever met off the Internet. I expected you to be homelier, I guess."

"Yeah, me too," I call out as I wipe my ass.

"Well, I'll be right back. I'm going to drop this suit off, OK?"

"Yeah, OK. I'll be fine in here." I climb into the steamy bathtub. Man, do I need this.

Years after Gusto, when the opportunity finally did come for Stacey to actually get married—to someone else—she made sure she found the longest aisle and the whitest wedding dress my father's money could buy. She was determined to recapture the dream Gusto nearly shattered. She stretched her walk down the aisle into fifteen or twenty glorious minutes of uninterrupted romantic bliss. A roll in the hay would have been so much cheaper, and probably quicker.

I watched her face as she made her way from the back of the cathedral, one tiny Barbie step at a time, her Barbie wedding dress dragging noisily behind her. I began to realize how important her dream was to her. It was indeed the most perfect bridal entrance anyone could possibly imagine. For those few brief minutes everything really did make sense. She cried the sacrificial tears for all the brides who would never be as happy as her; tears for all the times she had been the maid of honor—never the bride. We all cried with her. There was no trace of worry in Stacey's face—no care of what life after Barbie might be like. I cried too, mourning the tragic loss of her childhood.

I was a senior in high school by that time. This was during my all too brief romance with Jami. She was there at my side to appreciate my tears. Women are such suckers for men who cry. At the reception, she caught the bouquet. In response, I snatched the tossed garter from the hands of a small boy. The band played, "Sweet Georgia Brown," as I lovingly worked the garter up Jami's sweet leg. I kept that garter until just last week when I discarded it along with the rest of my things, eliminating any remaining evidence of my past life.

THE FISHFLY

I hear the front door opening. PJ is back from the cleaners. The water has gotten cold. I climb out and dry off. I put on her bathrobe and leave the safety of the bathroom. PJ sits me down on the floor in front of the sofa, facing the stereo, which is playing the music of Enya. She tells me how she is an ordained minister. She tells me her full title is, "The Right Reverend Mother Breastworthy of the Church of You Can Have Your Cake And Eat It Too." She says she's certain she can play the violin like Heifitz but chooses not to because she doesn't feel she should have to prove it to anyone, including herself. She tells me how guilty she feels, having abandoned her children when they were young and how her father died when she was twelve and how her grandfather died alone in his house and was found two weeks later, partially eaten by his seven cats.

Why do people feel they can tell me anything?

"I knew you were an intelligent man, by the way you write," she says. "Your letters have been very inspiring to me." She comes and sits on the sofa, behind my position on the floor. "You look a little tense."

"Yeah, I am kind of sore, now that you mention it."

She begins to rub me as she continues, "What were you doing in there just now, while I was gone?" That's an odd question.

"Nothing."

"Where were you last night?"

"I'll forgive you for asking if you'll forgive me for not telling you," I say evasively, hoping she'll leave it at that.

She reaches down and pulls my hand up and begins reading my palm as she massages it. "You will be reunited with someone from deep in your past." I pull my hand away, reflexively. *What did you tell her?* Nothing. She goes back to rubbing my shoulders. It really does feel good. "You smell so nice. I'll bet you work at it, don't you?"

"No, it's just your soap," I say, hoping she's not really the freak that the pit of my gut is telling me she is. She continues to ramble about her life, her children. She tells me her daughter is an epileptic. She mentions, almost in passing, how she has difficulty meeting her expenses. She tells me how she's always been accustomed to getting a lot of whistles from the younger men.

"My daughter says, 'Why do you put up with the harassment?' I tell her, 'When they stop whistling, then I'll know I'm in trouble.'" What the hell is she talking about?

Her nurturing shoulder rub has seamlessly escalated into a seduction. Her hands are now moving over my chest and stomach. She loosens the belt of the robe, while she continues to rub me with her warm, healing hands, which are incongruous with her manic ramblings. She maneuvers herself to the floor in front of me and goes down on me. No fanfare, no invitation, no resistance. Unobtrusively, she slips a condom onto my penis—almost too skillfully. I freeze in that old familiar way.

As she works her appreciable magic, I try to think of the right combination of words to express how awkward this is for me. Instead, after a pause, I tell her how lonely I've been and how delicious this feels.

I'm amazed how vulnerable I've allowed myself to be with PJ. After all, there's danger in the air. A woman I hardly know is holding my genitals firmly in the grasp of her powerful jaws. Tragedy or ecstasy is imminent. Which will it be? I cum. We lay there. Instinctively, she seems to know that it's time to rub me maternally. She seems to know the drill a little too well: Madonna, whore, followed by Madonna again. *What's going on here?* Something tells me I'm being played. *Why can't you trust anything?* The real question is why do I trust everything?

As she rubs, she expounds about her son, how he died of AIDS. He'd gotten pulled into the hardcore gay scene in the quarter. She describes the no-holds-barred sex parties where anonymous groups of men lock themselves into a room, with no one allowed to enter or leave for hours.

She leaves the room for a moment. Thank God, I need a break. With every new revelation I feel like I'm being drawn deeper into a particularly outrageous episode of the *Jerry Springer Show*.

She returns in a moment with a suit on a hanger. It's not my suit. "Your suit won't make it back from the cleaners for a couple days. This was my son's good suit. I want you to have it. I know it will fit you and I have no need for it."

"Okay..." I find my way into a standing position while I try to register what is happening. Don't they have one-hour cleaners down here? "Thank you, very much," I offer, instead.

"Are you allowed to bring a guest to this party tonight?"

"No, I don't believe I was invited to bring a guest," I say delicately. "Would you mind terribly if I took a moment to check my e-mail?"

"Sure, I'm not gonna stop you. Go on ahead."

I plug in; my Palm Pilot is craving a recharge. I insert the phone jack and open my e-mail. Bingo! I have a response from Gusto telling Flyboy that he can't wait to meet him/me in person. He suggests they meet on the riverfront behind the French Market at the Governor Nicholls Wharf at midnight. *Perfect!* I have him now. I feel a surprising giddiness, *the one bad guys always feel before they blow it*. I catch the feeling early enough, I hope. I rattle off a reply assuring him I can't wait to see him. It's hard to concentrate. As I try to write my reply to Gusto, PJ is handing me my clothes, one at a time, which she has folded neatly, warm from the dryer. I finish my note up quickly and hit the "send" button. I put on her son's suit. It fits me pretty well. I realize she's been talking to me for the last couple of minutes. I tune in:

"...and a lot of my friends have a sugar daddy. But I don't do my men that way. On the other hand, if someone wanted to help me out with my light bill or whatever, I wouldn't turn him down. You know what I mean? I have a lot of expenses, you know, fifty or sixty dollars would really help out."

It suddenly dawns on me what PJ is trying to tell me. She pokes her head into the kitchen. "What do you think, silly? You think sex is free? You think that's how it works? Well, it doesn't work like that. Not in the real world."

"It doesn't?"

"No, it doesn't. You want to go pick up a woman at a bar. You'll spend the same money on drinks and flowers and wine. And when it's over it's a crap shoot. Even if she does put out you're never sure where she's been."

"I'm not?"

"I mean you're a nice guy and I've enjoyed getting to know you. And you're more than welcome to stay here but I have rent and expenses to pay."

"You do?"

"Okay, cut the shit. We had some fun. Now it's time to pay the piper. It's as simple as that."

"I see."

"Yes. Take out that wad of cash you've got stashed away and let's get this show on the road."

There is a long silence as I go toward the bathroom to get my canvas bag. I indicate her son's suit by placing my hand over my chest. She nods her head in both approval and disgust and walks out of the room. I pack up the rest of my things, peel a hundred dollar bill off my "wad" and leave it on the kitchen table. I say my goodbyes to the patron saint of damaged goods and leave.

What has just happened? I wish I could tell when things were turning sour so I could stop them before they turn ugly. It's sad, really. Another relationship has ended before it's begun. I sure could have used an ally. But, on the other hand, I'm not here on a bridge-building mission.

Next stop, Rufus Hastings' home.

THE FISHFLY

I find my way back to the St. Charles trolley. I wait only a couple minutes. This trolley conductor has the same dead look I once saw on the face of a subway conductor in New York City, through the open door of his subway compartment. It was oppressively hot and stuffy that night on the *Number 4, Lexington Avenue Express*; I'm sure the open door felt good to him. It let in a force of hot, putrid air. Something in the way he stared down the tracks before him prompted me to lean in and initiate a conversation.

"Excuse me, how you doing tonight?"

He nodded, staring straight ahead.

I continued, "These trains go so fast. Sometimes I wonder, and I know this is a strange question, but have you ever, you know, by accident, run over a pedestrian with a train?"

There was a long silence as we banked a fast turn. He flashed a quick glance at me before he spoke. "In my fifteen years doin' this job," he stated simply, "my train's hit a person only three times and all three were homeless guys—y'know, vagrants." His face remained expressionless, his eyes never leaving the long dank tunnel of track in front of him. "The first time it was pretty rough. Second time, it upset me a little, but not too bad, ya know? Third time...the third time I didn't feel a thing. Not a thing."

I wonder if the man driving this trolley down lovely St. Charles Avenue could tell a similar story. He has a similar stare. He announces my stop and grinds to a halt. Our eyes meet for a flash as I step down from the trolley. I suspect the answer is yes.

My heart is beating hard in my throat now as I make my way down the oak-lined street to Rufus Hastings' house for dinner. I'm about to dine with Dr. Gusto Fernandez, a man who will be dead before morning if all goes according to my plan. I begin to imagine what it must have felt like to be the conductor of that subway train who no longer bothers to stop for "vagrants." I hope I too will be spared remorse when I do what must be done.

I'm pretty clearly not a violent man by nature. But I do believe, under the right circumstances, we're all capable of violence, even murder. After all, here I am, about to pull the wings and legs off a helpless fishfly. Correction: fishflies and vagrants are helpless. The creature I'm after is a cunning, vicious predator of the worst order. He feels no remorse for the damage he has done to me, not to mention the countless others whose lives he's undoubtedly ruined since. Gusto seems to believe he has the fundamental right to take whatever he wants no matter who he destroys along the way. He deserves his fate.

But in reality, the world is full of self-consumed sociopaths, following the cycle from victim, to predator and ultimately back to victim. I'm here to complete his cycle of despair and to free myself of mine.

Chapter 10
The Big Bully

I REMEMBER ABOUT TWO WEEKS AFTER my father's dramatic rescue of my Napoleon painting, a guy by the name of Kerry Fanning felt he had been my victim when I beat him out for first chair clarinet in summer band. This was back in July of 1974, between eighth and ninth grades. I didn't think it was a big deal. Predators rarely do. But I mean really, who cared about being first chair in summer band? Apparently, Kerry Fanning did. He was a year older than me so he had no business being in the *junior* high school summer band anyway. Not to mention, he sucked!

"I'm gonna kick your ass, Minello," he sneered in a low nasal voice, lisping his s's into z's, like some kind of a hideous reptile. He made several such threats in the days leading up to the summer band challenges. This was his last chance to take first chair from me. "I ain't gonna sit second chair to you, Minello. You dig? If I don't win tomorrow I'm gonna kick your ass." I was confident I would survive his challenge and didn't take his threat seriously at the time.

The day before the challenge I was alone in the band room, practicing. I don't think Kerry Fanning ever practiced, which explained why he was second chair.

I heard a sound. I stopped playing. I listened to the faint rumble of thunder penetrating the windowless band room. I remember a sick feeling, deep in my gut, which I had not yet learned to ignore. Was it my intuition warning me of the impending danger? I went back to my repetitions of scales and arpeggios.

Then suddenly, there he was. It turns out he'd been standing around the corner listening for the half-hour or so I'd been practicing. He announced his presence by thumping his fat paw on my left shoulder. I turned around in slow motion. My eyes locked onto his like a deer caught in a shiner's headlights. He easily lifted me off my chair and pressed me against a sousaphone locker. I held my clarinet firmly in my left hand, oddly afraid more for its safety than my own. I went limp, in typical fashion.

At this proximity, the pores of his scaly skin were considerably pronounced. At a distance, his face seemed so much more rubbery. I rifled through my memory in search of any voice that might provide a solution to my predicament. My father's artistic chiding popped into my head: *Squint your eyes. Get the big picture. See the forest for the trees.* But I was griped by fear. All I could see were the details of the leaves. I couldn't help marveling at the accumulation of white goo in the left corner of Kerry Fanning's mouth and the hideously large pores in his skin, like a million dirty orifices. I didn't want to see such details so I squinted my eyes even tighter, forcing myself to see the forest for the trees. With my eyes nearly shut I could only see the egg shape of his head and the sockets of his eyes. I studied the large masses of light and shade. Then, before I was able to stop myself, I asked in a most polite, almost patronizing tone, "How do you justify your existence?"

I think this caught him, and me, by surprise. He stared blankly at me for a moment, cocking his head slightly to the left, like a dog. Suddenly a key turned in the lock of the band room door. Luckily for me, Mr. Utrech had forgotten his umbrella. Kerry Fanning let me go. But I was sure my comment only threw salt in his wound. He would be back to finish what he started.

That night I went to my father for advice. "You've got to be prepared to fight if push comes to shove," he preached. "Otherwise he'll take you for an easy mark and you know what'll happen then," he prodded.

"What?" I asked, trying hard to follow his line of thinking, without provoking him. I really wanted to know the answer, even though I didn't really understand the question.

"You'll *become* one."

"Become what?" I probed, wanting to forestall the harsh assessment of my character that appeared to be forthcoming.

"An easy mark, what are you, deaf?"

"What could I possibly do to stop him?" I implored. "He's bigger than me."

As if on cue, my father launched into the pivotal story of his life. "When I was your age I had to walk two miles out of the way to get home from school. You know why?"

"No. Why?

"It was to avoid running into a very large thug of a kid. This fellow had marked out a certain stretch of New York City turf as his own. I had to walk an extra sixteen blocks out of my way to school every day, just to stay out of his way. Then one day I finally found the courage to take a stand in the face of uncertainty and danger. I found myself cornered by this bum, this Goliath. I don't remember his name anymore. But I can still see him."

My father looked up into the mental projection of his adversary's eyes. He re-experienced, right in front of me, the totality of all his fears, past and present, real and imagined. They were all wrapped up into what he referred to henceforth simply as the *Big Bully*.

"The *Big Bully* lunged toward me," my father continued, with a forceful gesture of his hands. "I had to think fast. So I rolled onto my back," he recalled, gesturing dramatically toward the ceiling to the sense memory of his nemeses. "And meeting him with my feet, I flipped him easily over my head and onto his behind." I listened in awe, my mouth agape, as usual. "From that day on no one ever dared pick on me again." He jabbed his finger into my collarbone for emphasis, just like Mr. Ballard. "Unless you stand up to the Big Bully you will never be a man."

The words "you will never be a man," echoed in my head for a good fifteen seconds. But then I thought about his story. How could *all* the big bullies of the world possibly know not to pick on my father? Did he just turn on a beacon of some kind, warning them he was invincible? Where did he get this supreme sense of confidence? What was the mechanism at work? How could I tap into this power?

It's hard to imagine in today's world anyone daring to risk a hand-to-hand fight to settle a dispute. Nowadays your opponent's likely to pull a gun on you, for Christ's sake.

We've become a society that wallows in man's inhumanity to man. We live in fear of the unknown, the most terrifying fear of all. That's the secret weapon of terrorists. Our country was founded upon this ubiquitous fear of the Big Bully. We've built our whole culture around being the underdog. Sometimes I wonder what would happen if there were no Big Bullies to fight. What if the Big Bully were part of a conspiracy of fear being exploited to control us?

"C'mon, I'm going to teach you how to make a fist," my father announced to me. "Lemme see you make a fist." I folded my fingers neatly together. "No, keep your thumbs on the outside or else you'll break 'em."

"Why do I need to make a fist at all?" I reasoned. "Just show me how to do the judo-flippy thing."

He answered by dancing around me like Mohammed Ali, jabbing at me and shouting, "Keep up your guard! What are you, some kind of a sissy?" After a few slaps and jabs about my face and midsection I just went limp; I looked down at my feet. He stopped and sighed deeply. "What's the matter with you, aren't you even going to *try* to defend yourself?"

I muttered, "I don't believe in violence." He stared contemptuously. I continued, "I mean, what if we could take all the money and energy we spent on war and violence and death, and spend it on life?"

"That's a bunch of malarkey," my father bellowed. "That's the kind of naive, liberal crap your mother's always spouting." It's true, my mother was an ardent liberal, back in the good old days before "liberal" had become a dirty word. That's where she was, after all, while I lay in my crib covered in shit. She was working for the JFK campaign. In retrospect, I could think of worse things for which to have been abandoned.

But I knew this egalitarian world view hadn't come from either of my parents. My pacifism came directly from the breathtaking ideas burned into my psyche as a devotee of *Star Trek*. The words I'd spoken were a quote from, "City on the Edge of Forever," one of the most profound episodes in the *Star Trek* cannon. It dealt bravely with the issue of being a pacifist in the face of near unanimous support for war. Kirk and Spock had to go back in time to prevent a particularly persuasive passivist, Edith Keillor, from delaying the U.S.'s entry into World War II. In this alternate future, that delay allowed Hitler to capture the world. Kirk's conclusion: "pacifism was the right idea at the wrong time." I wonder what Jesus or Gandhi might say to that.

None of this was of interest to my father. He and I sat side-by-side watching each installment of *Star Trek* during its first run on prime time. Ironically, while I was divining my personal value system he simply marveled at the special effects. He loved to theorize about how they created them. "Ya see that?" he shouted, applying the same intensity with which I grappled over existential self-examinations. "That was time-lapse photography!"

For me, *Star Trek* was a personal wellspring of hope to which I clung when I was growing up. It was the closest thing I had to a religion. My father raised us to be good agnostics. That is until I got "saved" at a Jack Van Impe rally. My next-door neighbor's mother insisted that I go. This was a few months before the summer of '74.

As I listened to Jack Van Impe's stream of non sequiturs, riddled with bible verse footnotes, my palms began to sweat. His blinding diatribe brought me to the conclusion that I was going to burn in hell for a very long time if I didn't get my ass down to the altar *right now*. I hadn't really considered eternity before that moment.

When I approached the altar for the prescribed laying on of hands, I felt an overwhelming feeling of relief from the emptiness I couldn't put a name to before that moment. I was prostrate, on the altar, my eyes closed tight, squeezing the tears of alienation and regret down my cheeks. Finally, I belonged.

My conversion, though fervent, was regrettably short lived. When the prayer was over, I looked up into Jack's metallic, blue eyes and somehow knew I was being duped. There was something calculating and sinister in his gaze. I just couldn't buy into it.

But by this time I had come too far, so I went along with the charade. My justification? I figured being saved couldn't hurt. After all, what if they were right? On the other hand, true faith is never blind and should never go unchallenged.

Star Trek was much more elegant a model. Each week highly advanced humanoids dealt with real conflicts, learning to embrace their humanity, while getting on with the delicate business of exploring the galaxy. They accomplished all this while taking pains not to intervene in another planet's development. Non-interference was, in fact, Starfleet's "Prime Directive."

The Christian religion seemed to be based on the exact opposite premise: proselytize or burn. I've always been suspicious of any idea that depended on me to sell it. Why would a movement as sweeping as Christianity need me on their sales team? It sounded like multi-level marketing to me.

With *Star Trek* there was Captain Kirk, who profoundly felt every crewman's death. He always rose to the task, overcoming every obstacle. He commanded the *Enterprise* with his intelligence, his cunning, his wit and above all his human intuition and compassion, "scratching his way to the top," as he put it.

Clearly, peaceful coexistence with other civilizations was a worthwhile goal in and of itself. Naively, I once believed that one day we frail humans might actually evolve into self-actualized entities and achieve peace among the diverse beings in our universe. Eventually, we might rise above mere tolerance and learn to embrace our differences. I longed for this universal acceptance of all things. I guess I should have gone to a Buddhist rally instead.

"The trouble with you is," my father's voice rudely re-insinuated itself, with the stern conviction of a Klingon, "you think you've got all the answers—well you *don't*! I'm trying to help you. If you learn to *defend* yourself you won't ever have to be afraid of anyone. Just like Teddy Roosevelt used to say, you've got to 'talk softly but carry a big club,'" he said, shaking his clenched fist, emphatically.

The principle of using aggressive force to *defend* one's interests is the moral justification for any good war. We feel it is our right, our duty to defend the "American way." Why is it that governments can wage war with impunity but if an individual kills, it's called murder? Our legal system takes this duplicity one step further by executing criminals for murder, which, by example, advocates murder as a completely acceptable way to settle our disputes.

We're always coming up with noble-sounding euphemisms to justify our wars. We call them "police actions" or "humanitarian missions." We're always "protecting national security." Why is it that standing for peace has never been patriotic? Unfortunately, when I was a fourteen-year-old peacenik, I was in no position to argue with my teachers or our government, let alone my father.

But in the end, after the last layer of truth is peeled away, I can't help wondering if my desire for world peace was really just a cover for a fundamental flaw in my character, an inherent lack of courage. Or is it just possible my reluctance to fight was based on a truly noble principle, worthy of enduring the risk and ridicule of others—like the Big Bully or even my father?

I was confused. What would Captain Kirk do? From my left shoulder came Dr. McCoy, in his gruff voice: *You can't turn your back on what you know is right. Sometimes you have no choice but to fight. If you let Kerry Fanning see your weaknesses he'll never stop.* From the other shoulder came Mr. Spock: *Logic dictates that violence will always lead to more violence. My people came to terms with their violent natures centuries ago.* There was Captain Kirk, turning away, tortured, overwhelmed, wringing his hands, *I...can't...make... the decision.*

"What you should have done is kicked Kerry Fanning's ass weeks ago," my father lectured. What were you afraid of?" He was right. What's the worst that could have happened: bodily injury, ultimate humiliation, abject failure? Nothing could be worse than being a coward in my father's eyes.

I wanted to just disappear, to go someplace where such dilemmas weren't so insurmountable. I wished I could have just beamed up to the U.S.S. *Enterprise* to hear, firsthand, Captain Kirk's orders when he finally snapped to his senses—because, eventually, he'd always know exactly what to do. But for some reason Captain Kirk's certain voice never weighed in on the subject. Perhaps he couldn't break through the din of lesser voices fighting for brain time.

So I made the decision to fight the Big Bully, whatever it took. I began by making a fist, thumbs on the outside. With practice, I found it possible to sustain this fist for several hours at a time. In my bedroom I began punching into the air. With practice, I learned to box, turning my hands into weapons of perpetual readiness. Anger became my friend. I spent the hot days of August punching a bag and sparing with my father, wearing provocation into habit. I began to look forward to the day when I would knock the proverbial chip off my very own Big Bully's shoulder—just like my dad had done so many years before.

But for some reason Kerry Fanning never turned up. The summer wore on. Maybe it was fate. Maybe the energy I was putting out into the world had somehow intimidated him. Maybe it was that by now summer band had ended. I'd heard he'd given up the clarinet altogether. On one level I began to feel sorry for him. But on an even deeper level I couldn't help feeling cheated, denied the opportunity to prove myself to my father.

I was a different person now. I had committed myself to conquering the deep-seated fear Kerry Fanning had so blatantly revealed in me. This fear, and the anger covering it, was as palpable to me as the smell of his sweaty body pressing me against that wooden sousaphone locker. It seemed ludicrous that I had once let this creature intimidate me.

As I sat alone in my room my imagination wandered uncontrollably, projecting a vision of two futures. In one, I reveled in the self-righteous satisfaction of beating the shit out of him. In the other, I groveled humiliatingly at his feet, a willing slave to him, and to my fear.

Physiologically, there is very little difference between

feelings of humiliation and self-righteousness. Simultaneous scenarios of both failure *and* triumph were surging through my body. These contradictory emotions were spinning around inside my abdomen, creating an almost sexual surge of energy.

    I became obsessed with asserting my supremacy over the legions of Big Bullies lurking under any rock I could find. And yet I still wanted to run away and hide. As it turned out I probably should have just watched more *Star Trek*. With all that self-righteousness and humiliation pulsing through my body, almost any incitement would be enough to merit retribution.

Chapter 11
Annie Sanders

WEEKS HAD NOW PASSED SINCE MY original altercation with Kerry Fanning, but I was still burning with resolve. This was the hottest day of the summer: exactly 98 degrees, inside and out. I had to get out of the house.

I decided I would just go over to Kerry Fanning's house, call him out and take him on, once and for all. The sidewalks were as hot as my determination to set Kerry Fanning on his ass. I crossed Twelve Mile road over to Violet Street.

But I never made it to Kerry Fanning's house. Instead, I ran into Annie Sanders, who was leaning against a beige Corvaire parked in the driveway of her house. Annie had been my first girlfriend—back when we were both in sixth grade. It was an innocent romance, the kind one might expect of twelve-year-olds. We used to just sit quietly for hours. She'd run her fingers through my hair, which I found completely intoxicating. The feeling was what I'd imagined my mother's touch might have felt like.

Sometimes we'd swim in her pool. Once, after a swim, I asked if I could sketch her. She looked so pretty with the sun refracting on her dripping wet skin. I remember trying to get her to stand in profile. I wanted future generations to know that when I was twelve years old, I had a girlfriend with nicely protruding breasts.

Things became more complicated between us in the fall, after junior high school classes started. Unfortunately, while she did indeed have extremely fine breasts for a twelve-year-old, this was nullified by the fact that she had become a very high maintenance girlfriend. It wasn't so much the wheelchair or the leg braces, which she had to wear every now and then because of the occasional surgeries to correct a minor birth defect in her knee. It didn't bother me that I had sort of become a nursemaid for her, pushing her around from class to class in her wheelchair. In fact, if anything I was perhaps a little too proud of the *idea* that I was taking care of her.

No, what made Annie a high maintenance girlfriend was that she always was finding ways to humiliate me in public. For example, while I was rolling her down the hall between periods, in front of everyone, she once complained, "God, Don, I don't mind your following me around all the time but do you really *have* to stare down my shirt? I mean, what a lech!" She was an embarrassment, alright. I had to let her go.

A year and a half later, in June of 1974, Annie Sanders and I would meet again at the annual band booster barbecue. It was between the end of school and the beginning of summer band. We were alone and offered to walk her home. What the hell, it was on the way. By that time we had just finished eighth grade and she was wearing lots of makeup. She looked like a hooker: very heavy mascara and lots of base. Why a pretty, voluptuous fourteen-year-old girl would feel the need for all that makeup was beyond me. By now she had developed quite a little reputation as a slut. Rumor had it that she'd already done it with Steve Corelli, whatever "it" was. I remember feeling angry at myself for finding such a vicious rumor so titillating.

As we walked, our pace slowed to a halt. Just before we rounded the corner to her house I asked if she would sit with me for a minute, even though we didn't really have anything to talk about. As we sat there on the curb, waiting for the streetlights to come on, I found myself wrestling with some very powerful hormonal urges. Apparently she did too. Before I knew it we were kissing, tentatively at first. But we kept on kissing. Something told me we weren't in Kansas anymore. They weren't just my first wet kisses. These were pulsing, nerve-wracking vats of warm communion with my primordial ancestors.

I found myself giving in to what was clearly her considerable experience. My tongue mirrored hers, moving slowly at first so as not to offend her with my lust. These kisses progressed into something only remotely related to what I'd heard other people describe as kissing. I could actually feel her body throbbing against mine, even through our clothes. It was so consuming and delicious, the hotness in my throat, the ache of lust in my groin, the intoxicating conflict between right and wrong. We were only fourteen, after all. And good Christians just don't do this kind of thing. The moral eroticism and physical chaos of it all made me more present and alive than I'd ever dreamed I could be.

I felt a bizarre kinship with the fishflies, which were swarming around the streetlights in dense clouds. Something told me they had the same frenzied ardor running through their primitive minds as I had. A few of them managed to tangle themselves in Annie's umber hair. Their large, transparent wings glimmered brightly in the light. Their fish smell was thick in the air; it was the peak of their short season on earth.

Fishflies live only twenty-four hours, long enough to copulate and provide a light snack for a hungry perch. This is their entire reason for existence; they are basically fish food.

1974 was a year of profound over achieving for fishflies. Thick swarms of them crackled like bubble wrap on streets as cars drove over them at night. They gathered in dark clouds around streetlights. They were dying in such deep piles near the lakefront areas of St. Clair Shores that in the distance Annie and I could hear them being shoveled up by the town's snowploughs and carried away in dump trucks. Both the fishflies and the trucks were now in operation twenty-four hours a day.

Annie and I paused for a moment from our kissing. It was surreal. "I think I love you," I said, my teenage lust beating hard in my throat.

"Me too," she replied. I swallowed arduously, gripped by a powerful, pounding, sexual single-mindedness. Telling her I loved her was the only way I could think of to justify what might, hopefully, be coming next. It made perfect sense: since we were "in love" we should *make* love.

Amazingly, she agreed. The plan was simple: she would come to my house the next day. No one was ever home, except my father, who would probably be working in his studio, oblivious to the outside world. William and Stacey were hardly ever home. So when Annie came over we would quietly go downstairs to my brother's old bedroom and do it. She and I agreed we'd go all the way. After all, we were in *love*. Of course I didn't have the foggiest idea of what "going all the way" actually entailed.

I didn't even know what to do with an erection when I was by myself. The mechanics of sex were still a sordid mystery to me. Perhaps she might show me the way. All I knew for sure was that I was going to have sex and that's all that mattered.

It was the perfect plan—except for the unfortunate fact that for some reason everyone in my family was in the kitchen, which was adjacent to the back door entrance. Stacey, who had just graduated from high school, was baking chocolate chip cookies, which she would never let us *see* her eat. William, a year older than Stacey, was beating hard on the piano with a muscular brilliance that resounded through the entire neighborhood. My father was cleaning his brushes in the sink.

It was into this domestic tranquility that Annie Sanders appeared, right on time, in a pink halter-top and red hot pants, lightly rapping at the back door. She looked like a goddamned candy cane.

I don't think anyone even noticed her. Even if they had, I can't imagine how they could possibly have known about our licentious plan. Yet for some reason I recalled images from *The Rise and Fall of Adolf Hitler*, a book I'd read in the fourth grade. Hitler apparently was fond of ordering women to defecate on him before shooting them. I imagined myself being discovered by my family in the middle of some unimaginable sexual act with Annie Sanders. I panicked. I could feel my face turning red, my throat drying up and sticking closed when I tried to swallow. In my mind, lust and shame had become inextricably linked.

I didn't want to arouse suspicion. Calmly, I moved to the back door before anyone could discover what was going on. I snapped open the screen door and stuck my head out, diverting my eyes from hers. Without revealing any part of my conflicted emotional state, I muttered, "I can't come out right now." Then I just let the screen door snap shut.

I watched as her big black caterpillar eyes fell downward. She cocked her head slightly to the left, as if she had been slapped in the face. After a long pause, she turned slowly to leave, her head bowed, her little ass wiggling sadly as she limped pitifully away.

This was now the first time I'd seen or talked to Annie Sanders since that inauspicious day. The fishflies had long since died in heaps and been shoveled away, along with any hope of my having sex with her.

She was wearing leg braces again. Apparently, she'd had

another surgery. What a pitiful picture she presented. Her whole demeanor seemed to suggest that everyone else was responsible for her bad luck. She had found the perfect balance between entitlement and self-pity.

I might have assumed she'd be bitter. By now she'd probably pegged me as a "typical male." The voice of reason chimed in, *You couldn't help it if you were afraid of what your family would think. Aren't you allowed to have second thoughts about throwing your virginity away on a tramp? After all, she'd already done it with Steve Corelli.* I'd known the truth all along: I only wanted to use her for sex. It was never my intention to have a relationship with her.

Even through the heavy mascara I could see in her eyes she had decided to seize this, the hottest day of the summer, to punish me for leaving her high and dry. But I was ready for her. My fists were coiled into what had become a semi-permanent clench. *You don't have to stand for any crap from her*, said the voice of assertiveness.

She gave me one of those forlorn, "poor me" looks. *What's that all about? You didn't do anything to her*, came the voice of reason. *You don't owe her anything. Your little romance was nothing more than a lot of big talk between two kids for God's sake!* Maybe I should have just ignored her. Why did she have to be outside today, of all days?

"What's your problem?" I snapped.

She pretended to be shocked, then whined, "You're the one with the problem. The trouble with you is you don't think you have any problems."

What nerve. Well, I wasn't about to go along on her little guilt trip. I had my own problems to deal with. I could hear my father's raspy voice, urging me to boldly speak the words he'd so often spoken to me. I gave his words a voice. I told her, "You got a chip on your shoulder, and I'm gonna knock it off!"

She responded, "You think you're so tough. Well I've got news for you. You're nothing—you're just a big *nothin'*."

Where did that come from? How could she know that about me? *Are you going to let her get away with that?* cried the voice of primal rejection. *I mean, where does she get off?* asserted the defiant voice of my father.

I told her, "Look, it's not my fault you're *crippled.*" That stopped her cold. I had never referred to her with the "c" word before this moment. I could tell she wasn't used to that kind of honesty—particularly from me. The trouble with her was she'd been mollycoddled all her life.

She called out, "Mom. Can you come out here? I need your help. Mommy! It's Donny Minello and he's picking on me!" She began shuffling toward the side door of her house.

You have to stop her, the voice of panic kicked into the conversation. *After all, it isn't your fault she's afraid of the truth. Besides, whatever problem she has with you should stay between you and her. Her mother's got nothing to do with this!*

I shoved her. She fell. I panicked. I ran. It wasn't right. I know. But she asked for it, didn't she? I mean, what was the big deal, right? I was sure she was okay. That's why she was wearing braces, to protect her if she fell.

For reasons I didn't question at the time I grabbed handfuls of dirt as I ran and ground them into my clothing and skin. I scratched the dirt into my face. I wanted to erase myself. I was scared, confused, overwhelmed with guilt. Something had gone terribly wrong. I didn't know what to do or where to go. I just knew I wanted the safety of home—to know that I was loved, unconditionally. I remember the rotten-food sickness in my bowels that made me feel more alone than I'd ever felt before.

When I got home, there was my father, calmly working at his easel. He seemed so serene, analyzing shapes, abstracting them into magnificent expressions of form. I waited patiently for him to finish the passage he was working on. He was deftly constructing a man's sleeve with his Series 52 Windsor Newton sable. Each stroke was a statement of himself, carefully thought out and executed with love, certainty and economy. When he finally looked up and saw me standing there, disheveled and out of breath, he put down his trusty brush with the reverence of an eremite. Spinning slowly, his chair squealing like a haunted house door, he looked me calmly in the eye and asked me what had happened to me.

"I fought the Big Bully, that guy I was telling you about? Kerry Fanning? Well, I beat him up," I stammered. "I faced my 'will to fail' and I—"

The phone interrupted my brave tale before it had begun. He swiveled back and rolled his chair to his desk as he sang into the phone, "HELLOOoo... This is he," and "Yes, I am," and "Yes, he's standing right here," followed by several sober "uhums." Finally he apologized and said calmly, "I certainly will... Uh-huh... Mm-hmm... Thank you for calling... I will."

He hung up the phone and looked downward, as he'd done so often when he was ashamed of me. With a heavy sigh and a long, still pause he infused the moment in my memory forever. Then, finally, his chair creaked and moaned as he swiveled slowly back to face me once again. He didn't look me in the eye. He was looking through me, his eyes perceptibly moist, his disappointment pulling me downward, like the gravity in hell.

A sick calm fell over me. There was an inevitability about the moment. The obvious was now astonishingly clear to me: I was the real Big Bully—not at all the lover of peace I'd believed myself to be. Who was I kidding?

My darkest thoughts and feelings had turned to action. There was no longer any question in my mind: I was culpable for the worst cruelties of mankind. All the sleazy daydreams, the guilt-tossed sleepless nights, the bizarre fantasies, were all a foreshadowing of my destiny. It all made sense to me at that moment. All my supposed virtue was just a slick self-deception, a puffed-up mirage to justify my inherent lack of character and integrity.

I moved toward my father very slowly, as if being pulled

along a supermarket conveyer belt. And as I lay myself across his lap, yearning for just one last childhood spanking in a feeble bid to wash away my guilt, I understood that the biggest bully I would ever face was deep within me all the time.

The spanking never came. I just lay there, draped across his lap, until he smelled the spaghetti sauce burning on the stove. From that day forward I was always prepared to exact my own punishment, an endless downward spiral of self-annihilation.

Chapter 12
6:52 p.m.

I PROCEED THROUGH THE FRONT GATE of the Rufus Hastings mansion. The flickering gas lights guide me up the walkway. I arrive at the top of the sprawling porch steps, passing through the huge, white, arching double doors, the kind with the large, non-functioning handles in the middle. Everything's big.

I am greeted with a glass of champagne, which is quickly placed into the one hand that doesn't know what to do with itself. It's as if I've been beamed into the opening scene of *Gone with the Wind*. Rufus has managed to gild every flat surface in the place. The sky-blue, silk-lined lemur drapes puddle thickly to the floor, a symbol of wealth in the old South. The lilting of a variety of southern dialects and the tittering of laughter fills the air.

There's my portrait of Rufus, the master of the house, looming serenely over the proceedings. The strong, dark features of the painting belay the charming persona of the man himself. It is both welcoming and foreboding, like an enigmatic gargoyle. It's the first thing we see as we enter the grand hall with its marble floors and twenty-foot ceilings. I am struck once again by his blending of color and texture, his attention to detail. A diamond-studded clock sits on an alabaster-topped key stand, next to a miniature painting of a distinguished old man. A cigarette box sits open on a sideboard, filled with blue and gold-leafed filtered cigarettes in perfect rows.

The door swings open behind me now and I hear the low tumbling laughter of Gusto, in response to the warm, lyrical welcome of Rufus. They make their way toward me, arm in arm. He introduces my adversary to his guests along the way.

"Gusto does medical research in the Brazilian rain forests. He assures me he will find a cure for cancer before I contract it. He's quite the heroic figure, isn't he, Donatello?" They stop, face to face with me. *That's your cue, asshole.*

"How exciting, Doctor," I say with just a little too much pause between "exciting" and "doctor." I'd read all about his 'cure for cancer.' It's all a front to lure little boys into his harem. I go along with the farce. "I've heard all those brilliantly colored frogs and poisonous lizards make for wondrous cures."

"It's a bit more complicated than that," he responds, condescendingly. "And please, call me Gusto." The motherfucker wants me to be his pal! *You can be his friend in hell, where you'll both burn for eternity!* How nice of Jack Van Impe to make an appearance!

"Exactly how do you extract their lifesaving venoms and secretions, Doctor Fernandez?" *Shut up about this dribble.*

"Please, I insist, call me Gusto," he says with an eerie firmness. My stomach wrenches. He explains, patronizingly, that the venom extraction is the easy part. Like I give a shit.

As I pretend to listen, I see her, appearing directly to his rear. She walks right in the front door. Astoundingly, it's the girl in white. She's wearing a more respectable outfit now but there's no question this is the same girl, the one from this morning. *What is she doing here?* She behaves as if she belongs here. *Call off the plan.* It is her. *Get out while you still can!* I was right. She is Rufus' daughter. *GET OUT!*

Oh Jesus, she's holding my sketchbook!

Rufus glides in between us. "And this is my daughter, Alicia. Donatello, I'm sure you remember her." I do remember. I DO. *How could you not have seen this coming last night? Abort the mission, asshole,* cries the voice of panic. *She knows too much! They're all in this together!*

"How could I forget?" I gently take the delicate hand she has offered me, playing along with the absurdity, the lackey in my own waking nightmare. "You're all grown up," I say, both to the girl in white *and* to Rufus' exquisite daughter, Alicia—both one in the same.

She seems to be trying to speak to me with her eyes, but what is she saying? Subtly, she indicates the sketchbook in her hand. Is it a warning? *She's taunting you.* No, I can't tell if she's angry or embarrassed. *She going to blow your cover. What did you tell her about your mission?* Rufus tugs her gently away and introduces her around to the other guests.

I've got to find a way to get her alone. If ever my dysfunctional intuition could tell me what to do next, now would be the time. But until I know for sure what's actually going on I will assume my plan is still a go. *Good, you've got to kill him, tonight! It can't wait. No, abort while you still can!* I wish I could shut off the voices screaming their opinions in my ears. *Confess your ridiculous plans! Take Alicia away! No, make a run for it!*

Cool it. We're staying. I mean, *I'm* staying. I'm here to see this through. *What if this is some kind of a setup?* True, what if there's a reason she's sought me out? Her life's got to be pretty crazy too. *No, you're the only one with problems.* But look at her. She looks as lost as I feel. For some reason I suddenly feel an overwhelming urge to tell her everything's

alright, even though something's telling me it's anything but.
"Will you be joining us for dinner tonight, Alicia?" Rufus prompts, a half-degree colder than his usual self.
"No, I've already eaten. I won't be joining you tonight. Thank you," she says, averting her eyes from him. There seems to be tension between them. What is it? I wonder. *Why should that concern you, asshole!*
Rufus takes a closer look. "Are you alright, darling? You look like you're going to faint. Prissy, get our little darling a glass of champagne," he says to the most effeminate of the three African-American menservants in his employ this evening.
"I'm fine," Alicia asserts. "Really." I could be wrong but I don't get the feeling she has told her father about our rendezvous last night. *Never trust your feelings, they have always betrayed you!* She hasn't once made eye contact with him. She has, on the other hand, made several attempts to steal a glance with me. Is she trying to tell me something? I wish I could read her mind! Where's Spock when you need him?
Of all the people I could have gone home with on Mardi Gras, I ended up with the grown-up version of Alicia Hastings. *She obviously knew who you were all along,* says the voice of logic. *But how could she have found you, let alone recognized you through all that confusion at the airport?* inserts the voice of the skeptic. No question about it, she must have deliberately sought me out during all that chaos. She must have gotten my flight information from Rufus and followed me from the airport. But why would she go to such lengths? And why didn't she identify herself to me last night? I need to get some answers before I take this any further.
The effeminate servant, dolled up in a little French maid's dress, has returned with another glass of champagne. In a loud, shrill voice, he snaps, "Yas, sir, Missa Hastings." He serves me champagne in a Venetian cut-glass goblet, inlaid with an intricate gold floral pattern. He may as well have added, "but

I don't know nothin' about birthin' no babies." My guess is Rufus hired him strictly for atmosphere. He spills champagne on my sleeve.

"Prissy, darlin', be careful," chides Rufus, patronizingly. "Be careful of Mr. Donatello's lovely suit."

"I'm sorry, Mr. Rufus," squeals Prissy. "I'm never gonna get it right."

"It's alright," I interject. "It's just good to be among old friends again," I toast, cheerfully, seizing the moment to both change the subject and ingratiate myself into their enigmatic world.

Eventually, the twenty-odd guests in attendance this evening, an assortment of mostly lawyers, doctors, judges, and other professionals, move into the dining room and are seated at a massive mahogany table.

I think about the long search, the many tentative attempts I've made to find the man who is now taking his seat across from me. We all strike up scintillating conversations with one another, in anticipation of what will undoubtedly be a sumptuous Lenten dinner.

Seated to my left is a priest. I wonder if he knows that Gusto has planned a sexual tryst with a young boy at the end of this evening's festivities. Could the priest actually be part of all this? Nothing would surprise me anymore. What might seem implausible anywhere else seems altogether conceivable in this paradoxical universe.

An immense centerpiece of curving, polished silver, draped with unnaturally large orchids and leaves, arranged without regard to cost, obscures my view of Gusto. Rufus' old, blind Chihuahua struggles to find her way down the center of the table, sniffing here and there for something appealing to eat with her one good tooth. One or two of the guests express visible disapproval; I catch Rufus making mental notes of who probably won't be invited back next time for supper.

"Poor old Mary Hastings," says Rufus with a dry, mocking

lilt. "She's looking for love in all the wrong places." Rufus takes the hands of the two gentlemen to his left and right and nods to Father Frederic, who defers with a nod to Gusto, who proceeds with the grace.

Without any prompting, Gusto asked my family to take one another's hands. He said grace at our family's Thanksgiving dinner back in 1974. This was the first time anyone said grace at a family meal. William and I would never have had the audacity to suggest such a thing, even though by this time we were card carrying "born-again Christians."

William got saved at the local Pentecostal church a couple months after me. He knocked over seven pews when his demons were "cast out." My sweaty-handed conversion seemed downright feeble by comparison. Neither of us had the nerve to tell the rest of the family about our religious disorders for fear of being ridiculed. Ridicule was fine for the apostles. They didn't have to live with my family, who regularly ate sentiment for dinner, particularly religious sentiment.

Maybe that's why we were so caught off guard by this pious man. We were all starving, not just for the turkey and mashed potatoes—Stacey had, as usual, cooked more than anyone could possibly eat—but more for the sense of decorum and grace Gusto was so unflinchingly feeding us. Gusto had class; we didn't. We glanced at one another in amazement as he stood up at his place at the table, slowly bowing his head, lulling us into a trance. My chin touched my chest, as if made to do so by a force beyond my control. Actually, it was my father, kicking my leg under the table.

My sister thought it was a good sign that Gusto wanted to spend "quality" time with our family, particularly with her little brother. She figured it proved his intentions were beyond reproach. He was reaching out to us, forging deep personal ties with each member of my family.

Gusto "beseeched" God's grace, asking for His

"deliverance" and "counsel." He spoke for what seemed like a full half-hour about world peace and the power of love and family.

"Give us the strength to cross the threshold of doubt, together, resisting with courage the temptation to judge one another. Give us the wisdom to recognize Your plan for us, oh Lord. Help us to understand Your love, Your perfect will. We are Your children and we ask You to be with us now. Make us humble in the presence of Thee, oh Lord. For there is a universal love which binds us together as we struggle to know what is right and good and just."

On and on he went, as our food cooled to room temperature. He was a perfect orator and the perfect boyfriend to my sister, projecting a purity and magnanimity she had only dreamed possible in a man. It was the ideal platonic romance.

"He's a faggot," declared Russ Raining, in his perfect staccato Chicago accent behind the Dairy Treat next to our school. That was the funny thing about Russ. He'd never even been to Chicago, but somewhere along the line he had latched onto this odd urban persona. It was an amazing affinity. But because he was undeniably speaking his heart to his best friend I was compelled to set him straight.

"You don't know what you're talking about," I lectured. "He's *involved* with my sister."

"Is he fuckin' her?" he pressed. I hesitated. "Well, is he fucking her?" Russ could be very belligerent when he got stuck on an idea.

"I don't know, Russ. It's none of my business."

Chapter 13
7:20 p.m.

MY DIGRESSIVE REVERIE IS BROKEN BY the voice of Rufus, calling to me from my immediate present. "Boy. Boy, I'm talkin' to *you*." Apparently, Grace has ended. Rufus has created a hush with his voice. "Now that I have your attention, boy, I'd like to enjoy your sweet voice, after your long absence. Donatello's been off in New York, trying to get into Carnegie Hall. Well, Donatello, have you figured out how to get there?"

"Practice," I groan, dutifully.

"Mr. Donatello, you do know, before you partake of these morsels we're going to make you sing for your supper."

I demure. He protests, encouraging his guests to take his side. They do so, without hesitation. And so we play out the old ritual of the South, a careful mix of humility and bravado. Eventually, I oblige, in accordance with the unspoken rule: Yankees must atone for the crimes of their ancestors committed during the "War of Northern Aggression." I do my part, as the most conspicuous carpetbagger in the group. Believe me, I can turn on the charm when necessary.

I had an excellent role model. Alicia's father is the mother of all charmers. Back in Savannah it was he who taught me the value of understatement in the delivery of a song. I can only imagine all the broken hearts, male and female, he undoubtedly has left in his path. His charisma is truly ingratiating.

Rufus tinkles his little bell and Dante walks in from the kitchen and takes his place at the magnificent grand piano at the far end of the dining chamber; I take my position in its armpit. I nod to Dante, who is dolled out in a white bow tie and a black tuxedo. He plays an elaborately arpeggiated introduction to "Somewhere Over the Rainbow." All eyes turn to me. I pray to the vast assortment of carefully placed religious icons all around me that I am in good enough voice to pull off this part of the plan. After all, it's been a while since I did anything like this.

As I sing, I scan my internal drive. All systems are functioning—my *instrument* is responding pretty well. Oddly enough, it feels good to release some of my pent-up energy into the music; it's about as good an excuse as I can find to move my anxiety through, and hopefully out, of my system. If not for these occasional moments of self-expression, I probably would have gone insane years ago. When I sing, my anonymity seems to bask in the limelight. I feel free. I allow myself to become Judy Garland as I sing, longing for a better world, somewhere over the rainbow.

Somewhere into the second verse my eye is drawn to a slight rustle behind a long velvet drape leading into the parlor. The corner of Alicia's face appears from the shadows. The people at the table, facing me, apparently do not realize she is there. Discretely then, I turn it into a love song for her; a vision of what might have been. My voice quivers. I feel flush. My lower lip begins to tremble. *What, you're not gonna start bawling?* barks the voice of panic. *It's OK,* allows my inner acting coach, reassuringly, *no one can determine the object of your feelings from behind the lyrics of a song.* As an actor, I'd trained long hours to wear my heart on my sleeve—to be present in the simple reality of the moment. No matter where I might have been emotionally, I was assured my secret was always safe behind someone else's words.

But all my training hasn't prepared me for a moment like this. I am pouring myself into the music, releasing all the uncertainty, fear, longing, lust, disgust; I'm inviting everyone in the room to emotionally undress me. Ironically, in a way, performing is a little like being raped. Yet despite all that's happened, or perhaps because of it, I find myself feeling more alive than ever before. *Stop. Don't give in to your feelings.* I fight the urge to weep. *Follow the emotional logic of the song. Tell the story. Just let go.* I manage to hold myself together well enough to finish the song.

After an unnaturally long pause, I receive a warm applause. Then comes the obligatory chatter about how multi-talented I am. After my mandatory display of modesty, I discretely ask if I may be excused to go to the bathroom. Rufus jingles his bell and summons Prissy, who glides in through the door to the kitchen. "Would you escort Mr. Donatello to the little boy's room? He needs to unwind after that electrifying performance. But don't be too long, Mr. Donatello. We have several courses before the evening is out. I hope we can prevail upon you later." His guests chime in with suggestive laughter.

Prissy leads me away, up the spiral staircase through the upstairs hall. More magnificent antiques and gilded paintings. "Missa Rufus is really happy to see you agin," Prissy volunteers lyrically. "I can tell. He never say those nice a things to any of the other boys he has singin' here." Great, now I'm part of his harem.

"Well, we go way back, Rufus and I," I respond, hoping to win trust wherever I can.

"Dat's what he say. I think it's really sweet, you comin'

back an' all. That's all Alicia ever talk about is you comin' back to us."

"Really," I prompt.

"She a very shy girl," he explains. "But she talk about you a lot."

"What does she say?" I venture.

"She think you are the cat's meow. She say you are going to set everything aright."

"What does he mean 'set everything aright'?"

"I don't know, Mr. Don. She talk a lot in code."

Prissy and I arrive at the door of the marble encrusted bathroom. This is no "little boy's room." I turn to Prissy and excuse him with a nod; I smile, as if to tell him, *It's OK, I think I can find the toilet from here.*

As he disappears down the stairs, I make my move, opening every door I can find. So many doors, so little time.

This must be Rufus' room. It's the most elaborately decorated bedroom I have seen in my entire life. It would make a great showcase for the gilders union. Think Liberace, add good taste and multiply it by fifty.

I go directly to Rufus' nightstand. There I find, as I'd hoped, a gun in the top drawer. It's loaded. I tuck it into my suit pants—all according to plan. I haven't come this far to stop now.

As I make my way back toward the staircase, I hear a sound coming from behind the door directly across the hall from Rufus' room. *Leave it, you got what you came for.* Slowly I walk over to the door. I press my ear tight against it and listen. I hear a TV playing inside. It's the unmistakable sound of porn, the generic jazz, pulsing under the generic grunts and moans of bad actors faking empty orgasms. The door is locked from the outside. The key's in the hole. That's odd. Quietly, I turn the lock and open the door a crack. There, in a canopy bed is a teenage boy, blond, naked, covered only by a sheet to his waist.

He turns his head toward me, slowly, like the last scene

from *2001, A Space Odyssey*. His dark, God-like eyes stare directly into my soul. The blue flicker of the TV dances in his eyes. The room is musty, stuffy. I smell that smell from years ago. That sickly sweet medicinal smell of K-Y jelly. My stomach wells up inside me. I close the door and lock it. I lean on it until I can catch my breath and balance.

Onto what madness have I just stumbled? The tinkle of clanging champagne glasses and laughter from downstairs adds fuel to my sensory spiral. I take a moment to gather myself up before I return to the party.

"He's a faggot," barks Russ Raining's voice interrupting my present. My mind snaps back to that day at the Dairy Treat. Thanksgiving break was over now and I was well into the autumn of my fourteenth year. That night was to be the last football game of the season; we'd made the playoffs. Russ was the undisputed hero of Rodger's Dodgers. In fact, he had used his considerable influence with the coach to get me on the team. I can assure you it wasn't my talent as an athlete that kept me playing. The only thing I had going for me was a certain tenacity. I was actually quite proud of how far I'd come since the August football camp, but I had no delusions.

Russ had the absurd idea that I would be able to keep up with him as an athlete. I was his very first friend and apparently this meant something to him. Even though we had little in common anymore, he was, in his way, fiercely loyal to me.

We met when we were only three years old. We both had just escaped from our respective backyard enclosures of hurricane fences and dull metal gates. Our paths crossed on the corner of Taylor and Champine. He was wearing a Superman costume; I was sporting a rather long hairdo for the period. My prophetic first words to him were, "Look, it's Superman!"

His response was, "It's a Beatle." Naturally, I thought he meant the bug.

"I'm telling you, he's a faggot," he repeated, turning to his left, revving up his piston-like laugh for all the other kids near the Dairy Treat to hear. They turned their heads toward us momentarily, and then back to their lunchtime repartee. I tried to adjust our stance, hoping to point our conversation in a more discreet direction.

"No, he's not a faggot," I hissed, trying to get him to lower his voice. "He's a gentleman to my sister and he just happens to appreciate me for my talent. What's wrong with that?"

Russ laughed louder yet. I realized, quite clearly, that it was a mistake to have mentioned Gusto at all. How could I expect Russ Raining to understand concepts like integrity, love and respect? Over the years he had become a stupid, cocksure jock out for a fast laugh at anyone's expense.

"OK, if he's not a faggot, how come he wastes his time on you?" I didn't answer. There was a silence. Then Russ fully extended his right arm and stiffly put his hand on my left shoulder. I had never seen such a sober look on his face. "Donny, there's two kinds of people in the world: boaters and golfers." Then he dropped his hand as if he had just revealed the secret to a happy life.

"Yeah…" I prompted, slowly. He seemed annoyed that I hadn't grasped the eloquence of his primitive philosophy.

"I'm a boater, Don," he added, as if adding that piece of information would make obvious the meaning of his previous statement.

"Yeah, OK…so what's the point, Russ?" I asked impatiently.

"Your friend Gusto?"

"Yeah…"

"He's a faggot!"

I wouldn't be able to appreciate his poetic insight until much later in life. Today, I can truly marvel at Russ' simple clarity. At the time, though, I was left to guess whether this was just another case of my missing the obvious or if there was indeed any truth in what he said. The bell rang. Russ turned and walked away, toward the school. Lunch was over.

Later that day, while pondering his words at the school pep rally, I felt a ripple, deep at the base of my rib cage. It was a small, almost incomprehensible voice, whispering the deeper meaning of what Russ was trying to tell me. He was right: something about Gusto was a little strange. He did seem to talk more on the phone to me than to my sister; he was much more attentive to me than to Stacey. What if Russ was right? What if he was interested in me, you know, sexually?

I just shook it off. There simply wasn't enough information to reach such sweeping conclusions. I preferred to base my opinions on facts and experience, not prejudice and narrow-mindedness. My relationship with Gusto was simply beyond Russ's ability to understand. After all, why shouldn't Gusto have been interested in me for my talent? I was an exceptional clarinet player. I was carving in alabaster, performing in plays, painting in oils, playing in sports. I was a straight "A" student. I was even popular, in my way, just having been elected "class clown" for the school yearbook. I had discovered endlessly clever ways of capturing the attention of others and earning affirmations from everyone but myself.

Chapter 14
8:13 p.m.

I FIND MY WAY DOWN THE wide, graceful staircase and emerge in the rear entrance of the dining hall. Rufus raises his voice a notch, without even turning his head in my direction. "And what are you giving up for lent, Mr. Don?"

"I'm sorry," I say, after a beat, "I was lost in the…in that exquisite painting behind you. Who's it by?"

"Peter Paul Rubens," he says, a bit too matter-of-factly.

"Wow. Nice. You don't see that every day. I'm sorry; you asked me a question, Rufus?"

"Yes. What are you giving up for lent?" All eyes have now turned in my direction once again.

"Fear. I'm giving up fear," I blurt.

This is followed by a short lull in the conversation; his guests seem to have some difficulty assimilating the incongruity of my answer.

"You know," says Rufus, changing the subject gracefully, "Donatello's painting of me is a masterpiece in the fine tradition of American portraitists, despite the subject matter. I asked him for the Dorian Gray special but he flatly refused."

"That would have cost you extra," chimes Father Frederic.

"Temperamental artists," continues Rufus, over the tittering. "But you know the little sketch he did for Alicia is just as precious to her, isn't that right, darling?" Alicia blushes, widening her eyes, subtly, as Rufus, again, without turning his head, directs all eyes to discover her peering in from the other room. "She has kept it with her all these years, Mr. Don—kept it close to her heart." The table rumbles with laughter and the sentimental sounds of "awww."

"Come on, darling, show Mr. Donatello the portrait he did of you when you were a little girl." Slowly, Alicia pulls from the front pocket of her jacket a tattered piece of paper, which she carefully unfolds. As she holds it up, the table fills with even more audible "oohs and awwws." But Alicia is not smiling. Her eyes are glazed with tears as she re-folds the sketch and puts it back in her jacket.

It's incomprehensible, that I could be so highly regarded by such a beautiful woman and never even know about it. *She obviously doesn't know you at all.* How could she? *You've betrayed her, after all those years.* I didn't know; I never realized. How disappointed she must be in me. I want to reach out to her right now. *Do it.* I can't. Not now. Not when I hold in my pocket the means to right the wrong I couldn't right when the righting was good. True justice has no statute of limitations, particularly when there is a deeper moral imperative at stake. Sometimes, inner freedom requires sacrifice.

I've sacrificed all my life. I have gone to plenty of psychologists, all of whom have tried to get me to move through my memories of Gusto. During my various therapies, I have reasoned with him, tortured him, embraced him, released him, sentenced him, even killed him. Most recently, it was

Marianne, a nun/social worker/psychologist/counselor. She made me imagine Gusto leaning against a wall. Through her prompting, she magically transformed an old mattress into Gusto Fernandez. She goaded me on. "He hurt you very deeply, didn't he? Tell him how you feel." She armed me with a foam bat especially designed for the business of purging demons. "Fuck you, I'm good enough," was the chant she coached me to utter.

Encouraged to repeat this mantra, I began a long crescendo of "Fuck you, I'm good enough." This escalated into a textbook-worthy primal scream. I began throwing myself against the mattress, repeating over and over again, "Fuck you, I'm good enough!" I became a nameless, frothing animal. "Fuck you, I'm good enough!" But was I?

The evening after the football pep rally, Russ sat next to me on the bus to Clintondale. The quiet throughout was breathtaking. Our ninth grade football team, Roger's Dodgers, was a well-oiled, victory machine in the home stretch of its most miraculous season on record. Up to that moment we were undefeated and un-scored upon. Even today, just saying those words, "undefeated and un-scored upon" sends a chill of pride into my ordinarily feeble posture.

This game turned out to be the only time our perfect record would even come close to being threatened. There were seconds left on the clock in the fourth quarter. The second string, affectionately known as "Donny's Dodgers," was getting some field time. I didn't know if the term meant I was the squad's captain or its mascot. Either way, we had somehow allowed a very tall, slippery halfback to break away. He sprinted 75 yards before Russ Raining, the only first stringer on the field and our most gifted runner, managed to catch up to him at the last second and bring him down on our *two* yard line.

Now it was first and goal. Coach Hanson bravely decided to

let the second string stay in, with the notable exception of Russ, of course, who was the star middle linebacker and first string defensive captain. Clintondale gained only six feet in three plays but they were now only inches from the goal line. On fourth and goal Russ called an aggressive defensive play, the "six-split." That was my favorite play because it meant Russ would join me as nose-guard on the line. The six-split works best with a nose-guard who's quick off the snap. My job was to "cover" the gap between the two linemen forming a defiant wall before me. With eight seconds left on the clock Russ and I glanced into one another's eyes, then dug our cleats down hard into the earth in a classic four point stance. Spontaneously, we began to growl at our opponents, portending my primal therapy sessions, later on in life.

There was an unbreakable connection made at that moment, between Russ and myself, which called to the heart of our friendship. In that instant I was able to give full expression to the hate and resentment I had bottled up inside me. Everything made sense now; it was the one time in my life I truly felt what it must be like to be in the "perfect will of Jesus." I took all the confusion, all the misguided longing and hurled it at the face of the poor kid in front of me. That's the genius of sports: the darkest, most violent human traits are the stuff of greatness.

I recall it now, in slow motion, as the ball was snapped. Immediately, I became aware of the gap, which opened up to the right of the lineman in front of me. Up until that very moment I had never really understood that I was supposed to get *through* that gap to the guy with the ball. As obvious as this *should* have seemed to the "captain" of the second string, it had somehow completely escaped me. At practice we crashed relentlessly and repeatedly into dummies. So I assumed this was what we were supposed to do in the game. This was then an epiphany of sorts, for me.

I lunged forward, lightly ricocheting off the left tackle and bouncing neatly through the gap. I batted away the opposing fullback like a bee and plowed headlong into the quarterback, who still happened to be carrying the ball. With the strength of a mother lifting a car off her stricken child, I drove that motherfucker straight back for fifteen yards before wrangling his worthless carcass to the merciless earth as the clock ran out.

No team ever came that close to scoring on us again and Donny's Dodgers instantly became an expression of virility and respect. I was no longer the mascot, I was a hero.

"We won," I yelled into the phone when Gusto called later that evening. "And guess what? I sacked the quarterback. They picked me up and carried me across the field."

"I'm so proud of you!" came Gusto's supportive voice through the receiver. "How does it make you feel?"

"What do you mean?" I asked, confused. I didn't want to miss what he was saying.

"How did your triumph feel to you?" he prodded, as if to push me to some deeper level of consciousness.

"It was exciting. I mean, it felt great." There was a silence. I heard a sigh. "Like what do you mean?" I asked, trying my best to get my answer just right.

"Your teammates, holding you over their heads, a man among men. All that strength beneath you, admiring you, loving you, enjoying you, enjoying your victory."

"It felt amazing. I felt so…taken care of. I don't know, it was just very…"

"Exhilarating," he prompted.

"Yes, it was like a dream."

"You know you deserve to have that feeling all the time. I know you, Donny. You give so much to others. You deserve love, to be admired, enjoyed." He spoke slowly, quietly. "I want to celebrate your victory." His words, the sound of his voice, felt good to me, like bathing in warm honey. Was this feeling sexual or was he speaking to a deeper need?

When I was fourteen, sexual desire was something that

happened in the hot, spinning agony of a dark, dank tunnel—a tunnel filled with angst and mystery. I had never had an orgasm, at least not consciously. I'd always regretted that I'd blown my one chance with Annie Sanders. The embarrassing fact was that I still didn't even know how to masturbate. No one had given me an operator's manual for my penis; it was like a creature from another planet. I felt so ridiculous. Was I supposed to have some innate knowledge, passed down from the apes? I really had no idea what to do with the damn thing when it got hard.

I remember late one night, kneeling on my bed trying to urinate through my tight erection. I longed for any kind of satisfaction. I knew something was supposed to happen, but what? I looked over my left shoulder. Through the curtained door, I saw my brother, William. Instantly, I plunged down into the mattress and pulled the covers over my head. How long had he been watching me? What did he think I was doing? I just lay there worrying what he must have thought of me afterward. We never spoke about it. How humiliating.

My only sexual satisfaction came in my recurring wet dreams. In one, I dreamt I was running away from a huge floating gelatinous blob that was trying to smother me. In another, I'd find myself floating face down on oceans of red gelatin. My nocturnal emissions were definitely exotic, if not erotic. If there were any juicy Freudian implications in them, they went completely over my head. I just assumed I was a sexual aberrant. Waking up on the cold wet spot was very upsetting. I'd just roll over to the dry side of my bed where I could safely fall back to sleep.

I still replay in my mind what it might have been like, had Annie Sanders come downstairs with me. In my fantasy, no one's home. We walk quietly downstairs to my basement bedroom. It's so cool and damp. There are no words. We embrace in a long horny kiss as we remove each other's clothes. Her halter-top unties without effort and slides easily down her back, revealing her full, young breasts, while my hands move over her hot pants, which have disintegrated like butter from the heat. Our mouths are inspired as they discover a new sense, deeper than sight, smell or touch. My mind travels through my skin into her body. We devour one another. Lost, we find our groins are connected. We're deep within each other now, floating serenely, disappearing into the warm liquid which has enveloped us.

    Back then, however, I simply begged God's forgiveness as I prayed myself to sleep, hoping to wake up in a dry bed.

Chapter 15
9:23 p.m.

THE SEVEN-COURSE DINNER HAS FINALLY COME to an end. The guests have been excused from the table, prompted by Rufus, who has risen first. I use this opportunity to look for Alicia. Everyone is exploring and admiring the numerous rooms in the main floor of the estate; I move through the little groupings, trying to find her. Instead, I am drawn into a conversation between Rufus, Gusto, and Father Frederic, who have broken away from the others. The four of us are looking up at the painting attributed to Peter Paul Rubens. It depicts a man protectively holding a boy to his bosom, shielding him from a light, emanating from the sky.

Rufus sips port from a delicately crafted, antique silver chalice and proclaims, "Everyone should have a wife, a mistress, a male lover…and a little boy." I laugh, reflexively, the way audiences sometimes laugh when a thing too absurd for words happens on the stage. I'm the only one laughing, though. Gusto moves a half step closer to me. "Think about it.

Did you ever wonder why it is that throughout history it has always been the men who've ruled the world? Alexander the Great conquered the known territories with an army of homosexuals. I bet you didn't know that. As lovers the soldiers felt compelled to protect one another more fiercely. This prevented more casualties and made for better warriors. There was a bond much deeper than that of brothers." He pauses and waits for a response. But I'm speechless. Instead, I finger the gun in my coat pocket.

Gusto continues, "Today they throw out the gays in the military, but the great empires in history were defended by predominantly homosexual armies. Yes, the proper Roman and Elizabethan gentleman always had a wife to keep titles and property, but the wife was never considered more than property, a pretty keepsake. It was his men that gave him power.

"Sounds a little chauvinistic, doesn't it?" I interject. I want to draw them out without appearing to be too judgmental of their untenable premise.

"Not at all," proclaims Rufus. "Women are absolutely essential to society. Don't get me wrong. I love women. I love everything about them. They are to be treasured, protected. Marriage is a sacred covenant. But, as with all God's gifts, our wives are intended to be enjoyed fully for what they are. Certainly, they occupy a place of honor. But so do our mistresses and male lovers. I made a joke a moment ago, but did you know, and I'm speaking historically now, that young boys have always been revered by the great men of history. Boys have always been a man's greatest love, his greatest treasure. There was nothing dirty or wrong in it. The affections centered on the youth have held the most powerful empires together. It was a well accepted form of mentoring for thousands of years. A man's love of boys was his way of passing his wisdom on to the next generation."

Gusto interjects, "Sex is power and it takes power to create an empire. All the great empires were founded on such mentorships."

"Are you saying," I stumble, agonizing to appear neutral on the issue, "that you believe sex between young boys and adult...men...is healthy?" *Shut up! Don't let on you're offended. Play the part, asshole! Go along with them!*

"Don't get him wrong, Don," says Father Frederick, "we believe in the adoption of laws that both protect children from unwanted sexual experiences and at the same time leave them free to determine the content of their own sexual experiences. What we are supporting is young people's right to emancipation."

Rufus steps back into the fray. "There have been numerous studies which have supported the fact that sex between men and boys was found to have had no negative influence upon the boys' sense of general well-being. Nor did the boys perceive in these contacts a misuse of authority by the adult."

In a bizarre tag-team-style banter, Gusto takes over. "In those cases where children do have sex with their homosexual elders, I submit that often, very often, the child desires the activity, and perhaps even solicits it, either because of a natural curiosity...or because he or she is homosexual and innately knows it."

I force my head to nod, as the words, "Oh, I see," fall out of my mouth the way brain matter fell out of JFK's head.

"What we are saying, simply," states Rufus, "is that for thousands of years, men have championed the young. It is a right of passage upon which we in modern society have turned our backs. Nonetheless, it is the natural order."

Okay, clearly there is no longer the remotest chance Gusto could have connected me, the man standing before him, with the boy he molested thirty years ago. Gusto seems completely lost in his convictions on the subject of child abuse. He thinks he's looking into the face of a prospective convert, but it is his executioner that returns his gaze.

What if I killed him now? The gun is warm in my pocket. I've been fingering the barrel while we've been talking. Killing him now would be so easy. I can imagine the blood pouring from the hole in his forehead, just like in that scene from *The Godfather*, where Michael Corleone initiates himself into the family business.

These three men are actually trying to convince me that pedophilia is a part of the natural order. As absurd as it is to believe, I am being groomed for membership in the North American Man Boy Love Association.

My eye shifts to a curtain rustling behind Rufus and Gusto. Alicia has been standing behind a curtain in the doorway to the parlor. Has she been listening to this entire conversation? I glance at her asking for an explanation with my eyes. Is she shocked by this demented scene? Surely, she must be used to hearing this kind of conversation. I sense an inner strength at war with a resignation to the strong will of her father. *You're reading into it. You have no idea what she's thinking.*

For the moment, we exchange a quick, seemingly knowing nod. She lowers her head and disappears back into a side room. I want to run after her. *Take out the gun and shoot Gusto. Kill him now!* I want to lose myself inside her. *Run away! Shoot yourself.* I want to take her away from all this. *You're a coward.* Yes, I want to throw myself into her arms and run away. *Why didn't she tell you who she was last night?* Did she assume I knew who she was all that time? *You're such a clueless jerk; how could you have not known it was her?* I'm sorry. *She's part of their secret world.* No! I want to hold her and protect her from these monsters. *Run away, coward!*

No, I can't keep running away from myself. I've run as long as I can remember. The deeper I've looked inward the farther I've strayed from who I am. I've been living a lie. I've convinced myself I was operating above the fray, that I wasn't subject to the same vagaries as others. *It's all lies.* Yes. *You're a monster!* I've been living a lie. *You're one of THEM!* No! I don't deceive innocent boys. *You deceived yourself.* That's true, I did!

I tried to bury my conflicting sexual longings in the Church. I joined my brother's church, Christ Gospel Tabernacle, a few months before Gusto ever came into my life. By the time he came along I was attending church three times a week, participating in weekly rehearsals with the "Redemption," our gospel band. During the whole ordeal with Gusto. I was even part of a ministerial training class. If I had completed the program, I would have been the youngest Pentecostal missionary in the state. Although the complexity of reconciling these distinctly separate lives seemed impossible, I had no choice but to find a way.

On one particularly sleepless night after a long moral roller coaster ride on the phone with Gusto, I prayed, as I often did, for the baptism of the Holy Spirit. Sister Samantha Dell, my pastor, had said to us, "Ask and you shall receive. Seek the way of the Lord and you shall find it. You must ask, demand if you must, for the baptism of the Holy Spirit."

I was waiting for the sky to open up and fill in all the missing pieces. I ardently wanted to speak in tongues like my Pentecostal brothers and sisters. I longed to commune directly with God. I desperately wanted to have a personal relationship with him. To me this meant actually seeing Him, hearing Him, not merely feeling Him. I wanted to be in His perfect will like all the others at church seemed to be. I wanted to know that simple purity. The more I prayed, however, the more aroused I became. The creature from between my legs fed on the guilt and anguish of my loneliness and confusion.

"I'm afraid it's time for me to take my leave," Gusto interrupts. "I want to get a good night's sleep before leaving for Brazil in the morning." I overhear him whispering to Rufus that he has an appointment and will likely be spending the night at his place in the quarter. *You've got to do it tonight!* Yes, I know. His farewells are warm but quick. He kisses each of us three times on the cheek and leaves.

The scrape of Gusto's five o'clock shadow transports me back in time to my first kiss with him, thirty years ago. It came after many long hours of wooing over the phone, but it still took me completely by surprise. Here's how it happened. It was about a week after the Thanksgiving dinner of 1974. Gusto, Stacey and myself were making a day of gallery hopping. The two of them seemed to enjoy listening to my scathing critiques of semi-professional art. Either I was impossible to please, or pickings were indeed slim in Detroit back in the seventies. Not that I had anything against all the splatter painting and assemblages of trash. I was a great fan of Pollack and Picasso. It's that I felt uninspired by the lack of intentionality and sense of resolution in most of the esoteric, pretentious crap on the walls of the galleries.

After taking in several of these ridiculous "non-profit" midtown art galleries, we ended up back at the Scarab Club, where the tired remnants of traditionalism found a welcome home. This is where my father kept his studio. The light before dusk poured through the lead glass panes of the French doors, leading from the main gallery to the garden. The bright orange beams were obliterating whole paintings with their phaser-like glare. Vernon, the white-haired caretaker of the club, was vacuuming the second-floor lounge, just above us. He was a very sweet, very old black man who had long ago accepted his place as a servant among whites. The soulful humming of his vacuum provided a musical underscore for the ensuing scene.

Stacey had gone to check up on our father, who was in his third-floor studio, organizing. He was always organizing but never organized. He accomplished most of his paintings in the middle of the night, creating his masterpieces like a dutiful monk.

The conversation between Gusto and myself had tapered

off. His words were spinning in my head. I can't deny it made me feel remarkably special that a doctor had taken such an intense interest in me. He appreciated my artistic insight and supported me in my frustration with the Detroit art scene. He told me again that in his country men were passionate about what they believed. "We believe that a passionate life is the only one worth living. We do not compromise. We trust our feelings." I honestly didn't think when he said "passion," that he really meant *passion*. Once again, the obvious had managed to escape my grasp.

"Yes," I said.

"Can I be absolutely honest with you?" Gusto continued.

"Of course," I said, eagerly.

"You and I are not subject to the narrow views of the mediocre people all around us. For you and I, there is a powerful destiny." The sun either went behind a cloud or set behind a building, changing the cast of the room from a burnt sienna to a cooler blue-gray hue. The moment was ripe and the soft hand of authority pulled my head toward his mouth. As his scruffy face twisted and scraped against my chin it felt like a spear shooting through my abdomen. I went limp with conflicting impulses. The feeling was undeniably powerful, though I couldn't label it. My solar plexus was dancing fiercely. What did it mean? I couldn't understand. *You're in dangerous waters. Get out!* said the voice of panic. *No,* said the voice of reasoned arrogance coursing through my veins like a tranquilizer, *you should be more open to new experiences. You feel more deeply than your friends. Why are you always afraid of what you don't understand?* All I knew was that I *felt something powerful* in my gut; it was the closest thing to adventure I could imagine, like being dropped from an airplane into the remotest part of the world and trying to find my way home. Was it possible that this is what it felt like to be in love?

In a moment my sister returned and we continued our cultural tour of Detroit's dilapidated art institutions. Stacey didn't suspect a thing. She seemed so far away from me, in her Barbie-like reverie.

The sound of Gusto's final farewells at the front door lurches me back to the present. *What are you doing, daydreaming? We've got business! You've got to get to the river before Gusto.*
As I slip into the front hall to make my exit, a pair of soft hands reach from behind a curtain and turn me gently to face their owner. It's Alicia. She pulls me into a side parlor.

"I've been trying to find you alone all evening," she whispers. "Why have you been avoiding me?"

"I haven't been. I've been trying to get to you too."

"We've got to talk," she whispers, firmly.

"Yes, we do. But I…I can't. Not now. I have to leave. It's extremely important that I leave, right now." The words falter out of me like a bad soap opera actor. I wish I could tell her where I was going—and why.

"But I," she begins, then shifts gear, "I wanted you to have this back." She hands me my sketchbook, without quite letting go.

"Is it true, what your father said?" I venture. "Have you really kept that picture I drew of you all this time?" *Of all the stupid questions you could ask…*

"Yes, I admit it. God, what's the big deal? I had feelings for you."

"Had?" *Don't push the subject, asshole!*

"Have. OK? There, I said it. I've always wondered about you, ever since I was a little girl. I know it's silly and now I feel really stupid. But what can I say? There was a connection. I feel a connection. I can't explain it." She pauses; she seems to be looking for some hint of reassurance in my eyes. "OK, I've said enough," she continues, finding none. "I feel completely humiliated. Are you satisfied? I could tell you obviously weren't interested in me when you walked out on me this morning."

THE FISHFLY

"That's not why I left." How can I reassure her without dragging her into my sordid plan? "It's just that I..." My hesitation seems to confirm her theory about me. Finally, she says, "I think you'd better go." *You're pushing her away, you idiot. DON'T LET HER GO! SAY something!* "No, please listen. I can't tell you why I left. You've got to trust me when I say I had to go when I did and that I've got to go now. Please, just trust me." *No, don't open up to her. Push her away. Don't drag her down with you. Get out, Gusto's getting away. You've got to stop him. No, stay. Let her in.* Stop! All of you!

"Why should I trust you?" she responds. "But then again, why shouldn't I trust you? I'm in no position to expect anything from you." *How can she be so generous to such a dissolute freak? What have you done to deserve this compassion?* I feel an overwhelming *fight or flee* response, emanating from my brain stem.

I move to leave. She stops me and locks her eyes onto mine. "I see someone who is hurting, like I'm hurting, and I want to help, if I can." *What planet is she from?* She's actually reaching out to me. *Why? What does she want? She must want something.* But she's seems so open hearted. *She's trying to maneuver you into a corner. Don't trust her!*

"But you don't really know me."

"But I *believe* in you. There's something in you. I don't know what it is. I saw it in you years ago and it's still there, just below the surface. There's a kindness...a sadness, under the hurt. Some kind of a window—a chance, maybe...a future. I know it sounds corny, but when I look into your eyes I feel a connection to humanity. I can't explain it."

That's it; she must be luring you into a trap. She's in on this whole thing, don't you see? No, she's looking right into my soul. I can see myself in her eyes. She's trying to soften your resolve. She's playing you for a fool. Don't let her do it. Get out! GET OUT!

STOP!

"I don't understand something. Prissy told me you think I'm here to 'set things right.' What did he mean?"

She gently places two fingers on my lips and shakes her head, quickly. "Look, meet me back at my apartment above my father's antique store, later tonight," she says firmly. "We have a lot to talk about. This isn't the time or place for it. I want you to know everything."

"Everything about what?"

She finally releases the book into my hand. She looks directly into my eyes. "Take this and go. I'll meet you later and explain."

I turn and walk away, finding my way out the front door with as few goodbyes as I can get away with. I can't believe Alicia wants to see me later. What does she need to *explain*? She said she feels a connection. *Don't believe her.* Is it possible for me to find love, considering the monster I've become? Will she want anything to do me once I've finished what I came here to do?

Chapter 16
11:13 p.m.

I BARELY CATCH THE LAST TROLLEY running to Canal. As we grind from stop to stop, I notice the people on the trolley are talking about a rare infestation of strange bugs, pointing to a front-page article in the paper. It says they had to bring in scientists to analyze the strange creatures. They've only just discovered what they are. Apparently, a huge infestation of fishflies has recently hatched in the river; this has thrown the citizens of New Orleans into a complete tizzy. Scientists have determined that fishfly larvae have somehow floated down the Mississippi River and hatched in New Orleans. What are the odds of that happening? *6,432 to*—Shut up, Spock!

If I believed in fate...that is, if, out of the chaos, there were indeed some higher power guiding the universe, then I might think He/She was trying to tell me something. The convergence of present events, after a lifetime of seemingly meaningless occurrences, must have some significance for me. But what is it? Why have fishflies reappeared in my life at this moment?

What are they doing in New Orleans? I try to recall my first experience with fishflies but I can't. It's as if they've always been a part of my life.

I reach down to open my bag. I need to write my racing thoughts into my Palm, but instead my sketchbook falls onto the floor of the trolley. A piece of folded paper, which seems to have been tucked into the middle of the sketchbook, has fallen free.

What is this? I pick it up; I unfold it. There is a CD inside. On the paper is the drawing I did of Alicia so many years ago. This package had been marking the final page of my drawings from last night. I turn it over. There is writing—not in my hand—scrolled into my sketchbook. It reads:

> Don, I could not say what I am about to tell you while we were in my father's home. For years I have been collecting information regarding his involvement with an organization called NAMBLA. It is a real organization and its members are everywhere. My father, as well as a number of the men with whom you ate dinner tonight, are part of a larger conspiracy of complacency to protect child molesters in the courts. Though not viewed as a serious threat by the mainstream, NAMBLA continues to exert great influence, under the protective umbrella of the American Civil Liberties Union, whose difficult job it is to protect everyone's rights, even child molesters. NAMBLA is making a lot of headway in the courts.
>
> This CD contains a database; I've been working on it for years. It exposes a network of prominent NAMBLA members, who are made up of lawyers, doctors, priests, judges and members of other respected professions. It details their connections to one another for the sole purpose of undermining and diluting rape-shield and other laws intended to protect the victims of child abuse in this country. They

must be stopped, Don. People have to see beyond the rampant deception in our judicial process to effectively change the systemic corruption, which continues to destroy children's lives.

The story you told me last night about what happened between you and Dr. Fernandez, it broke my heart, Don. Now, other people need your help. I can't do it alone. Whatever else he is, Rufus is my father. I can't be the one to bring him down.*

I slam the book shut and stuff it into my bag. *What did you tell her?* I must have been drunker than I thought; I don't remember telling her about Gusto. *You ASSHOLE, you are pathetic. You told her everything!* Not about my mission. *How do you know? You don't remember, do you?* She didn't say anything about my plan in her note. *She set you up!* But at least, now I know where she stands. She doesn't know about my mission. *You don't know that for sure!* I don't know anything for sure. *I can't believe you're so stupid you didn't see this coming. What are you going to do with this information?* I don't know. It seems she's on a similar mission. *But it's not your mission!* All I know is that I've come here to kill Gusto. *That's what you have to do.* I don't know what to do with all this NAMBLA crap and these conspiracy theories. I don't know how to feel or what to think about anything else except why *I'm* here. This is a personal quest; it's between me and Gusto. That's what's real for me—like the way I felt after Gusto kissed me in that molten orange gallery at the Scarab Club.

That evening, during what had evolved into a nightly ritual, Gusto reassured me, repeating over the phone to me that the customs in Brazil were different than ours. He told me there were many cultures who express affection differently than ours.

"Our differences are not something to be feared. They are to be embraced. I would never *impose* my culture on you, just as I wouldn't expect someone from your country to impose his culture on me. I'm sorry if I upset you tonight. It was insensitive of me."

"No, you were just being honest," I said, the affirmation catching in my throat. "I'm the one who should be sorry. I'm still just a little confused," I offered in a devastating understatement.

"I know you are. And I understand where you are coming from." He went on, "How can I explain this to you? Your feelings are perfectly natural. The fact that you can share them with me is proof we have a special relationship. In my country men often kiss one another; it is a sign of admiration and friendship. Trust your feelings. That's why we have them. Don't be frightened or embarrassed by them. You feel things intensely. You see into things more deeply. That's what I love about you. I don't think you realize how rare a being you are. There's no need for you and I to cede to others the ability to transcend the absurd mores of this repressed, puritanical society," he reasoned. "We are beyond that. If sex comes along, let it happen. We are under no obligation to conform to their limited world views. Just because you and I are more open to life than the others…" he added, trailing off, inviting me to fill in the rest of the thought. "How can we expect people to understand these things? Should we allow ourselves to be subject to, to be dictated to, by these…?"

"Well, these mores are so much a part of the way things are in this country…" I interjected, feebly wanting to sound insightful. I remember the feeling at that moment; it came upon me suddenly. It was the sensation of falling, of not wanting to hurt his feelings. Did he really say "if sex comes along, let it happen?" Or did I imagine it? I was desperately afraid of losing his approval, which had somehow become intertwined with my belief that I was exceptional, in some essential way. Nothing else he said seemed to matter. So, I nodded in agreement with him, adding quickly, "We're a society of sheep."

"That's true of others, but not for you and me. It's not easy to stand above the fray. It takes an unshakable courage. We must be free to dream, to soar. Look around; you can see the ocean of mediocrity. We stand above that sea, you and I. It takes courage to understand the ways of other cultures and the special connection we have." I was speechless. This sounded awfully similar to something my father once said to me. Gusto sighed, "I'm so proud of you." He closed in a whisper. "Good night…is it alright if I tell you 'I love you'?"

"Of course," I assured him, profoundly aware of the black hole I was climbing into, but too afraid to pull myself out of it. "I'm sorry if I seem so stupid and confused."

"You're not stupid, you're brilliant. You are an inspiration to me. That's what I love about you. Do you understand?"

"Yes, I understand."

"Do you feel the same for me, Don?"

"Yes."

"Do you love me?"

"Yes…I love you. And, Gusto?"

"Yes."

"Thanks for believing in me."

My trolley ride ends at Canal. I move into the anonymity of the French Quarter and quickly make my way to the riverfront. I feel the festive lights of the city fade into the darkness of the night as I walk down river toward the wharf Gusto told me I'd find. The clouds are low and moving fast. I feel as if I could touch them as they pass. The river is as black as the night, with occasional street lanterns marking the way for the nocturnal set. Swarms of fishflies flit in the lights, lending me some small comfort as I pass.

A gang of what appear to be homeless kids is scattered along the waterfront, standing on the rocks that fortify the shores of the Mississippi. I keep walking along the levy until, at the far end of the riverfront, where it disappears into the night, I spot another group of teenage kids hanging out very near the water's edge. They seem so matter-of-fact, so cool, so certain, casually flicking fishflies out of their long beaded hair and off their drab, hip-hop clothes. I think back to my teenage years and wonder how it is possible anyone lives to adulthood.

Chapter 17
Dan Garvey

"FUCK YOU," BULLIED RUSS RAINING, AS he thunked another humiliating Bipper—that's what he called it when he slammed his knuckle into Leonard Pinto's fatty head. "Try it and make history," squealed Leonard, bumbling out of a headlock and loquaciously moving into an effeminate swish of the wrist.

"You're a faggot," Russ barked at poor Leonard.

"No I'm not," Leonard snapped. "I'm just fuckin' with your head, Russ!"

"You better not fuck anywhere near my head, ya faggot," Russ said as he delivered another Bipper on the accented syllable of the word, "Who's fucking with whose head now, *faggot?*"

What was it with everyone's obsession with homosexuality? I knew sex between men wasn't normal. Perhaps in some cultures it was; how would I know? Apparently, it's been a part of our own culture for thousands of years, at least according to

Rufus, Gusto and Father Frederic. How was I to know what was normal? I only knew it wasn't normal in *my* culture. I had no way of knowing what normal was in Brazil or Rome or King Arthur's court. All I knew for certain was that the last thing I ever wanted to be was "normal." I wanted only to be exceptional. Just like Gusto said, "why should I cede to others the ability to transcend the norms of society?" I had no point of reference to judge the difference between normal and *healthy*. Gusto was the closest thing I had ever had to a role model and the word healthy never came up in our conversations.

The whole concept of homosexuality was only a dim abstraction at best. To me, being gay was an outside thing. Even the word "gay," as applied to homosexuality, was a relatively new addition to our vernacular in 1974. I never seriously considered whether I might be gay myself. Homosexuality was just a strange aberration that happened between men who found themselves failures with women. Back in ninth grade at James Rogers Junior High School, failure with women was easily explainable and dismissed: girls were either "sluts" or "snobs." Some were both. And my pals and I had no use for either.

By now we were the kings of junior high school, at least in our minds. I was a proud member of a loose association of fourteen-year-old boys who had no particular mission or creed. Downtown, these groups were more glamorously called gangs. Though the word suburban implied an inferiority to our urban counterparts, our "gang" much in common with the broods of teens who tonight wander peripatetically on the shore of the muddy Mississippi. They seem to depend on one another for their very survival.

The principal members of our "gang" were fat Leonard Pinto, the lackey, Johnny Bails, Mitch Dawson and myself. The others followed our lead. Johnny, Mitch and I provided color and intellectual justification for whatever escapades our leader undertook. Dan Garvey had by now outmaneuvered Russ

Raining to become our leader. Like Russ, Dan was a man of decisive action. If he thought it was time to get on our bikes and ride down the street in formation, we did it. Unlike Russ, who used intimidation and brute force to command respect within our gang, Dan Garvey used his wit, charm and style. Dan's more tolerant demeanor was better suited to our ragtag bunch of overachievers, most of whom went on to become doctors and lawyers. In retrospect, I might have characterized Russ's leadership style as absolutist, while Dan was a relativist. I for one appreciated the moral wiggle room.

In short, I felt accepted, even if not fully understood. Gusto, in contrast, seemed to take a much deeper interest in understanding me. Perhaps, in retrospect, acceptance trumps understanding.

It was Russ who was responsible for bringing Dan into our gang. The Garvey coup began the day Russ Raining talked me into going out for football in the fall of 1974. I figured football might be an excellent use for all that pent-up anger left over from my thwarted conflict with Kerry Fanning that summer. Not to mention, I was in pretty good shape after my father's summer boxing lessons.

Because Dan was not as gifted an athlete as Russ, he was relegated to the second string with me. Dan and I met the first day of football practice. We became fast friends when both our bikes were stolen during that fateful first day.

After my bike was stolen, my father made it clear he wasn't about to buy me another brand-new $120 Schwinn Varsity ten speed. So he gave me $40 to get whatever piece of junk I could find to replace it. I went to a police auction where I bought the first bike on the block: an old rusty Stingray with no brakes. It was perfect for doing "no-man-riders," which I performed with a reckless aplomb. I'd peddle the bike to its top speed, then jump off and tumble to a halt, launching my bike like an unmanned projectile.

One day I executed the perfect "no-man-rider," smack into

Dan Garvey's family's car port, shattering a couple of wood planks in the siding. That was the first time I'd ever been to his house. He didn't know exactly what to make of me. Evidently, he found me intriguing enough to become my best friend. I'd camp out at his house for days at a time. His family lived right on Lake Saint Clair. We'd spend hours sitting and talking overlooking the water, behind the sea wall in his back yard. Among the thousands of subjects we covered was masturbation. He did most of the talking. I listened and learned as he described over 84 ways he'd discovered to get off. Sixteen more and he could have written a book. My favorite was the one where he smeared Vaseline all over his penis, put a sock over it, wrapped it in a hot pad and lay a vibrator over the whole apparatus. "Then what did you do?" I asked, starving for his encyclopedic knowledge of sex.

"Well then I just put my hands behind my head and wait," he replied, matter-of-factly. He seemed to know all about sex. He'd had several juicy sexual encounters by that time. Chicks dug him. He had a way of drawing people into his world. I could only admire his powerful sense of self. I had none. I found myself unable to share my conflicting feelings with my best friend.

In that pivotal autumn, back in 1974, I was still operating without a map. Even after my talks with Dan the vagaries of sex remained a complete mystery to me. They wouldn't be for long.

Occasionally a story came down the pipe about someone who was supposedly a queer. But these were almost always rumors. One notorious exception was Tim Pebble, who was a year older than us. He was a *flamer* from the word faux. He was almost militant about his gayness. In fact, he boasted openly about his numerous homosexual accomplishments. He didn't seem to be the slightest bit interested in the stigma others attached to being gay.

One day he approached Dan Garvey, who was, as far as

anyone knew, a card-carrying member of the heterosexual party. On this day, however, Tim Pebble offered Dan twenty dollars to let him suck his dick.

"You're not going to let him do it, are you?" gasped Johnny Balis.

Confidently, Dan Garvey proclaimed it was "a no brainer. After all, twenty bucks is twenty bucks."

That was it. It was to be an event, with a small, invited entourage to act as a Greek chorus in witness of the lurid spectacle.

It was going to be a showdown, a test of wits and wills. Our gang showed up at the appointed time behind Shores Hall. It was four o'clock on that still, crisp September day in 1974. *Star Trek* would be on TV in an hour. Dan Garvey stood waiting, coolly leaning with his shoulders against the wall, his left leg bent, hooked on a slight protrusion from the cinder block wall, Jimmy Dean-like.

Onto the scene walked Tim Pebble, along with his fag goons, who stared humorlessly at the rest of us. Our gang stood fish faced, mouths agape, waiting for something disgusting to happen. Tim Pebble walked over and knelt in front of Dan.

"Well, whip it out, Garvey! What are you waiting for, a pussy?" lisped Tim Pebble. His fag goons chuckled, humorlessly. I noticed their Adam's apples seemed to protrude slightly more than the boys in our gang. I wondered if I had discovered a physical attribute that might help identify queers in the future. It was dead quiet. Dan looked directly into the eyes of his would-be-cock-sucker, then out to the gawking group of morbid gawkers. He seemed to be thinking twice about his fast twenty.

What started out as simple test of wills had became so much more. It suddenly dawned on everyone present that letting someone blow you was itself a homosexual act. True, Dan wouldn't actually be doing anything. But still. I felt a tension pulling in my chest. Wasn't anybody going to say something, do something to help our leader?

Dan Garvey thought deeply for a long moment, breathing in a long sigh and releasing it. Then, like a prize poker player, folding his best bluff, he shook his head in contempt; he simply turned and walked away from that twenty bucks and quite possibly the best blow job he would ever get in his life. He also seemed to prove, once and for all, and in the witness of those present, that he was no fag and never would be.

Chapter 18
The Seduction

MY MIND RETURNS TO THE PRESENT as I hear the faint echo of "Do you Know What it Means to Miss New Orleans" being played by a local cover band in one of the French Market cafés. As I maneuver myself to the end of the levy, I notice the breeze from the river has dropped a degree. I climb down onto the wharf and follow the moving pack of teenagers around to the Merion Street Warehouse. I climb up onto a huge cement slab where two tugboats are docked, the *Admiral Jackson* and the *Louisiana*. The homeless kids are still in view as I stand peering into the entrance of the vast empty warehouse filled with silence. Inside is only the occasional light, which creates a maze of murky shadows. The inside is at least three football fields long and smells like musty rubber.

Something in the odor wrenches me back to the evening of the incident between Gusto and myself. He and Stacy had planned a surprise weekend for us to go out and do "guy" things. He was going to give me the royal treatment, an all expenses paid vacation from my suburban doldrums. My family raised no eyebrows. There was no reason to. He was a doctor, after all. He had taken an oath to do no harm, for God's sake. He had been nothing but kind to my sister, to me, to my whole family.

That Friday evening, Stacey had cooked a huge vat of spaghetti for a dinner party put on for the doctors by the first year nursing students. She was in charge of her dorm's kitchen crew and was distraught because she had overcooked the pasta, or noodles as we called them back then. Ordinarily, Stacey was a pretty good cook.

I sat across the table from Gusto in the cafeteria. He seemed tired after a long shift. He blurted, "Don't eat too much of this crap. Remember, we're going out for some real Italian later." I was surprised to hear him talk that way about my sister's cooking. It wasn't like him at all. He made a fast recovery though. "It's not Stacey's fault, this is no way to prepare a meal." His jaw was so rugged and square. He wore his white doctor's smock with absolute conviction. But something in his demeanor seemed distracted, almost impatient. I hoped it wasn't anything I'd said or done.

Stacey joined us at the table, her paper plate barely dirtied with her handiwork; she rarely ate in public, preferring to do her binging and purging in the privacy of her own bathroom.

"So, are you guys ready for your big weekend?" My stomach suddenly felt queasy. I attributed the feeling to having eaten too much of her overdone spaghetti. I didn't want to tell Gusto I'd eaten a whole plateful before he arrived.

"Absolutely," came Gusto's response, a little too quickly. He seemed nervous.

"What are your plans?" Betsy inquired. Then, realizing she was meddling, she rolled her eyes and added, "Guy stuff, I remember. I'm sorry." *What do you think you will be doing all weekend?* came the cynic. *Don't worry, Gusto has big plans for the two of you,* came the voice of denial, reassuringly.

Finally after a few goodbyes, Gusto and I were on the road, driving in his brand-new, red Alfa Romero. As we drove, I became faintly aware of an odor I had never smelled before. Was it his cologne? It had a sickly-sweet, medicinal scent that I didn't recognize. I cracked my window a little.

Later, at Pasqualli's Restaurant, we sat in a booth against a wall of densely hung Chianti bottles. The maroon candle lantern between us gave the table a blood-red glow. The spell was broken temporarily when the waiter refused to bring the wine because I was obviously underage; can I help it if I was a late bloomer? With a restrained impatience, Gusto reprimanded the waiter. "I'm a doctor. Do you understand? This young man is in my care. Do I need to speak to the owner or were you going to bring me the wine?"

When the waiter disappeared to do as he was told, Gusto railed on the rampant incompetence and pettiness of wage earners, rule-followers and technocrats. "It's amazing how few people have the guts to risk the legal consequences of a moral act."

The wine tasted bitter but it made me feel very grown-up. "Yeah, what an idiot, that waiter," I added, with disdain. I couldn't believe how superior I felt in Gusto's company.

"I want you to know something. I'm not sure you realize that you're no less of a person," Gusto said, moving closer to the crimson candle in the middle of the table, "than any politician or doctor or the owner of this restaurant. I see through your short-sighted view of yourself, to your greatness." I'd stopped hearing statements like this as flattery weeks ago. I'd always suspected I was special. If only other people could see what Gusto seemed to see so easily in me. He was strong for me, a true friend.

I pushed down the sickness in my gut. On some level I knew what was coming but I desperately wanted to believe someone was right about me. Could the sensation in my abdomen have been an awakening to my true destiny or had I eaten too much spaghetti back at the hospital? He leaned in even further, positioning himself directly above the candle, so it lit the bottom planes of his face like Dracula. His noble features glowed menacingly in the flickering light. "Let me be your champion."

Later, after driving for what seemed like hours we finally reached his apartment, which was fine with me. I needed time to digest everything that was happening, including the second helping of spaghetti. We were in a part of town I didn't recognize at all. After we entered his front door, he locked the dead bolt with a key and put it in his pocket. I stopped breathing for a moment. *What did he just do?* Clearly, there was no going back now; I was completely at his whim.

The place was very clean, with white Formica everywhere. I smelled that smell again. It was much stronger now. It had a peculiar, medicinal odor. We sat on his couch. The wine had made me warm and smug. Who was I to judge what was right or wrong? Why should I worry so much? *Get out of here!* came a faint voice, nearly completely quelled. *Run,* screamed the voice of fear, like a distant siren. *Shut up,* came the confident voice of reason. *You're in the hands of an extraordinary individual, a doctor, for Goodness sake.*

We sat on his couch and smoked pot and drank more wine like two adults. We were enlightened. Superior. "My feet are tingling, Gusto," I said.

Gently he replied, "It starts in your feet and works its way up." He rubbed my legs to help the tingling along.

"You are a fearless soul. What is happening between us...do you feel it?" he cooed in my ear.

"Yes, well...I'm not sure," I replied. Some part of me still wasn't quite ready to resign to the inevitable. That's when he kissed me, the way he had done at the Scarab Club two weeks before. *Danger! Danger!* The red lights were flashing but now I couldn't hear the screaming of the sirens or the roaring of the engines. I didn't know what to do. I certainly didn't want to be rude or upset him. I had no idea where I was or how to get home even if I could somehow get out. No, I was here for the duration.

I felt astonishingly stupid. Clearly, I'd been wrong about everything; I wasn't exceptional. It was all just a trick to get me alone. I froze in that old familiar way. In a flash, my delusion of greatness was stripped away, just like the clothes that were coming off my body. In a moment I'd be naked, both physically and emotionally.

I felt the scratchiness of his face on my neck and chest as he unbuttoned my shirt downward to meet the tingling coming up from my feet. I knew that if I felt uncomfortable or wrong it was my burden to overcome, not his. After all, he had given me every warning this was coming and I had done nothing to stop it.

Chapter 19
11:48 p.m.

THERE HE IS. I SEE HIM now. It's Gusto, walking toward the gang of teenagers near the riverbank. He's early; it can't be midnight yet. I don't think he's seen me, though, so I watch him from behind a stack of metal pipes. I take off my suit coat and tie. I pull my black shirt and ski mask out of my bag and put them on, stuffing the evening clothes into my bag. I pull the ski mask securely over my face. Gusto approaches the teenagers on the far end of the wharf.

Suddenly, I hear a noise coming from behind me. A boy from the group of homeless kids has discovered me. The sight of my ski mask startles him. He backs away toward the riverside entrance of the warehouse. I move to cut him off. He stops. I look into his face. I see myself. His eyes are bright, despite the drugs he's apparently been using. He seems so sure of himself. "What's with the mask, man? Hey, wow, get it, *masked* man. That's totally cool."

"Those your friends over there?" I inquire.

THE FISHFLY

"Sometimes they are. I don't really have any friends. I was like totally into angst way before any of these dudes. Sometimes it's easier that way."

"Sometimes it's just lonelier," I chide. I want to shake him, slap him, hug him, wake him up, tell him everything will be all right. But I don't believe it myself.

He sees my gun. "Dude, what are you gonna do, kill someone?"

"I want you to do me a favor. There's money in it for you." I put two twenties in his hand. "There's more when you finish."

His eyes close as he slinks machinelike to his knees and moves to unfasten my zipper. "No," I reprove, firmly pulling him back to his feet. "Not that. I didn't mean...please, stand up. I need your help."

"What kind of help?"

"I need you to pretend to be...somebody else. You see that guy over there with your friends? I want you to tell him your name is Flyboy. It's a code name. I want you to lead him away from your friends. I want you to get him alone, on the other end of this warehouse, away from everyone else. Do you understand? I need you to keep him occupied until I—"

"You don't need to explain it, dude. I understand." He grabs his down payment from my hand and disappears into the shadows along the perimeter of the vast structure.

I'm so afraid. It's actually happening. It'll all be over soon. *You'll never get away with this. It's insane. Give up!* But I'm so close. *You're no killer.* Yes, I know. *You're a failure.* Yes, I am. You're right. What am I thinking? I can't go through with this.

I walk out of the warehouse, across a dark field to the street, toward the worry-free festivities of the French Quarter. I stumble onto a phone and call the police. *That's right, call the police. You don't have the balls to kill him. You'd never risk the legal consequences of a moral act.*

"Hello, I need to speak with a detective." *Wait a minute,*

what are you doing?

"Is this an emergency?" asks the tired voice on the phone. *Stop!*

"Yes. I'm standing a hundred yards from a known pedophile and I think I'm going to kill him." *Shut up! Shut up!*

"Have you filed a report?"

"What?"

"Have you filed a report?"

"No, I haven't. Listen, I want to turn myself in. I'm afraid I'm going to do something terrible and I need your help." *You're a big nothing!* "I want you to help me stop this man." *You're a pussy!* "I need you to send someone to arrest him." *You've always been a pussy!* "I want to prosecute him. He's a sex offender."

"Where and when did the incident occur?"

"What?"

"Where and when did the incident occur?"

"Thirty years ago in Detroit."

"Please hold." The voices are coming in hard now. *Hang up the phone. Be a man. You don't need the police. There's no justice in the legal system. They don't care about you. You can't give up now. You've come so far. Don't be a quitter!*

Shut up!

In a moment a man gets on the line. "I'm sorry, partner, this isn't something we can do anything about. Any statute of limitations has expired long ago in a case like this. Where did this happen?"

"In a suburb of Detroit."

"Hey, the Motor City!"

"Please help me!"

"Okay, okay. Now look. I'm sorry, there's nothing we can do for you."

"But I have him. He's here, right now, the man who—"

"Look, partner, why don't you come in tomorrow, in the light of day. We'll get you some counseling. For now, you just go on home. Get a good night's sleep. We'll look into it tomorrow."

"But he won't be here tomorrow. He's leaving the country early in the morning. You've got to come and get him *now*."

"Now just calm down. Let it go. We don't have any jurisdiction and we're up to our ears with cases like this—cases that are happening at *this* very moment. You're talking about ancient history, fella. We don't have any manpower to spare on this."

"But you don't understand—"

"Look, I've got to take another call. There's nothing we can do for you. Just take it easy. Go home and get some sleep."

He hangs up. Alicia was right. These people will never do anything about Gusto. What kind of feeble response to my cry for help was that? There is a "conspiracy of complacency." Well, I won't accept it. I CAN'T LIVE ANOTHER MINUTE OF COMPLACENCY!

I drop the phone, take two steps backward, turn and run back to the entrance of the warehouse. Now, from a farther entrance I can see the shadows of two figures moving next to a lone forklift, parked in the middle of the vastness. It's Gusto and the teenage boy. I can see them but I can't hear what they are saying. What are they talking about? The boy turns his back on Gusto, drops his pants and lays over the driver's seat of the forklift. Oh my God, what is he doing? Gusto is mounting him. *What have you done? You've sent an innocent boy into the hands of this monstrous pedophile. You're destroying him with your pride and stupidity.* No, he must have misunderstood my instructions. I wasn't paying him to have sex with Gusto! *Do something!* I can't.

I wanted to do something back then too, but I couldn't. I was his prisoner. After he removed my clothes I was too afraid to move or to resist. What would he have done if I had? Before I knew it my penis was in his mouth, just like Tim Pebble had wanted to do with Dan Garvey. *But he didn't do it—you did.* DON'T YOU THINK I KNOW THAT?

It was then I discovered the true meaning of self-hatred. I didn't know what else to do but execrate myself. I tried to make myself go away. *You enjoyed it.* No. Yes. I'd never felt anything this vile, this defiling, this overwhelmingly pleasurable in my life. The feeling in my stomach was sickening, yet somehow, the sensation of my first blow job blew me away. *You're a faggot!* NO! I was confused, scared. The feeling grew deeper and deeper. Then suddenly, my body convulsed in what was the first orgasm I'd ever had while awake.

And the night was still young.

Gusto's driving the boy hard now. I can't see his face in the shadows. *He's hurting him! Stop him, you coward!* I CAN'T! *You ARE a big nothing, aren't you!* I feel so helpless. I don't know what to do. *You know!* No, I don't. Yes, I *do* know. I know I'm afraid of what I've *got* to do next.

I was unable to speak for days after that weekend at Gusto's apartment. Nothing came out of my mouth when I tried. My father knew something was wrong but he didn't seem to know how to approach me with it. Finally, after a week of keeping this horrible secret locked inside, I walked into his room and sat down next to him. We waited in silence for several minutes. Eventually, I was able to tell him what happened.

That night, my father drove Stacey and me to Gusto's apartment. There, we confronted him, if you could call it that. I couldn't speak. I was still in shock. The last place in world I wanted to be was back in his apartment.

The tone of the conversation seemed incongruously quiet, even polite. At one point, Gusto offered to get each of us something to drink. While in the kitchen, from a position in which only I could see him, he hissed silent threats at me, pointing his finger, menacingly. My father, oblivious to Gusto's efforts to terrify me, calmly suggested he might have to call the AMA unless he agreed to stop calling me on the phone, which he had continued to do every night since the weekend of the incident. "I don't want to make trouble for you, Dr. Fernandez," my father reasoned with him. "But as you know, I'm getting married in a few weeks. You've put me in a terrible position."

Put HIM in a terrible position? What about YOU! I know. *Your father betrayed you—he fucked you just like Gusto did.*

But what about later? When we got home and we were alone again, my father asked me if I wanted to press charges. He didn't seem to push it, though, as if he was reluctant about making a big deal over the whole thing. It was as if he was urging me *not* to press charges. He wanted me to know about the inevitable public humiliation that would follow, pointing out prosecutions in cases like this were rarely successful. Child molestation was still not being talked about when I was growing up. Now, of course, it's a staple of daytime television.

"Why put yourself through all that?" he asked gently. *You know why. It was to save HIMSELF the embarrassment!* No! He was thinking of me.

"Maybe it would be best if we just forget about the whole thing. Why drag this all out in the open?" *He was saving his own ass. He was worried about messing up his upcoming wedding, his reputation.*

No, he was trying to make it easier on me!

His reputation was more important than his own son.

No, he was trying to shield me!

You're deluding yourself. He was still hoping Gusto would help him get that big portrait at Children's Hospital.

No! He wanted to protect me.

Your father let Gusto get away with it!

If so, I'd say I got my father back for his complicity with Gusto. It was only five years ago when his stroke took place. By then he was old and getting frail. Funny, how old age seemed to catch up to him suddenly. I was at the age when most men tend to forgive their fathers for their parental shortcomings. I swear that was my plan.

We were in his studio, going over some papers. I began telling him that I'd forgiven him for not standing up on my behalf, for not prosecuting Gusto. But I hadn't. It was a lie. Before I was able to finish, he bellowed back, "You've got a lot of nerve, bringing that up now. You're the one who insisted on keeping it quiet."

"I was a kid!"

"That's a bunch of malarkey. You were the one with the will to fail. Not me. You're always blaming somebody else. That's been your problem all your life. The trouble with you is—"

I don't know. Something snapped in me. Suddenly, I felt an overwhelming urge to let him have it. I wanted him to know what the trouble with me *really* was. I screamed back at him, with a primal viciousness far more intense than anything I'd ever achieved in therapy.

"The trouble with me? The trouble with ME? The trouble with YOU is you're a cruel, angry, self-centered son-of-a-bitch who never gave a shit about anyone but yourself! You didn't even try to save me. Your own son. You were too embarrassed to stop him. I was just a kid. You could have ended it right there. How many other lives has Gusto destroyed because of your inaction? Have you ever thought about that? You let him get away, Scott free!" I was raging by this time, out of my mind. "Your own son! You protected HIM instead of me. I was standing in the way of your getting that portrait commission at that hospital. That's all you cared about. AND I WILL ALWAYS HATE YOU FOR IT!"

I made a motion toward him—only to bring home the point. I wasn't going to hurt him. I would never intentionally injure him. I swear I never actually touched him, physically.

I stopped. Then he stopped, his eyes bulging, first in fear, then in agony. His face became white, then blue. He fell to his knees, right in front of me.

Chapter 20
12:37 a.m.

I CAN SEE A SIMILAR AGONY in the boy's face now as Gusto pounds himself into him. *He is destroying this kid, this little boy, condemning him to the same desolate future as you. Do something! Stop him. You have to kill him!*

I watch, frozen in self-loathing, as the other homeless kids discover what's happening to their comrade. They charge toward the scene. They pounce on Gusto, taking his wallet and beating him up and kicking him on the cement floor of the warehouse. I feel like I'm about to pass out.

What are you waiting for?
I'm afraid.
It's what you came here to do!
I know. But I can't. I'm so confused.
You're weak. Who are you to be avenging anyone? You're a worse monster than any of them. Because you're letting him destroy you.
I'm dead already.

Do something!
What if I fuck it up?
Risk is our business. Oh God, not Captain Kirk!
What are your orders, Captain?
I can't make...the...decision.
Please. Stop. I can't do this anymore.
That's why we're aboard here.
This is not real!
One day, no braid on my shoulder. A beach to walk on.
I'm going insane. *Are you relinquishing your command?*
Command of what?
You can't risk your life on a theory.
A what? Dr. McCoy?! Mr. Spock! What is happening to me?
No, this isn't a TV show. There is no such thing as Captain Kirk. This isn't a dream or a TV rerun of my past. THIS IS REAL.
Do something!
Stop badgering me.
KILL HIM!
STOP!
I lift the gun over my head and fire. The sound is deafening. It echoes for a long moment in the giant building. The kids scatter like roaches from a can of Raid. *What have you done? You're committed now.*
Committed to what?
Finish the job! You've crossed the line! You can't turn back now.
No, RUN! RUN! RUN!
You've got to finish what you've started. Do it!
Do what?
Do what you must do! This is your last chance!
What must I do?
KILL THE MOTHERFUCKER! KILL HIM!
Like a shot, I run toward Gusto, toward my destiny. The

faster I run the farther away he seems to be, like a slow motion nightmare. Gusto is trying to get up. He is hurt. They've beat him up pretty badly.

Good! Finish the job! Don't let him get away with what he's done! Kill him.

I won't let him get away with it.

Save us! Stop him now!

I will!

I stop a few feet from Gusto, at his feet. He looks up and freezes. He props himself up, one arm on the ground. My ski mask is doing the work I can't. He appears to be frightened out of his mind. I look into his eyes. He sees only a man in a ski mask, holding a gun. I wonder if he'd even remember me after so many years. I point the gun straight at his head.

Gusto holds his hands toward me, palms facing out. He is pleading for his life. In spite of my best efforts, I find myself identifying with him. I recall when I was twenty, a mugger pressed a gun to my forehead and demanded money. Thank God I had some. He took ten dollars and one electron from every cell in my body. *Shut up. This is no time for empathy.*

Gusto wasn't afraid of me then, when he had me, defenseless, captive in his apartment. After my orgasm, he maneuvered me so that I straddled on top of him. He sat me squarely on his lap, while he lay flat on his back below me. I remember the sickening sweet smell of the K-Y Jelly he used to enter me. That was the smell. The pain was excruciatingly evil. Like a darkening hell, my vision went brown, then almost black. I envisioned falling into an empty pit of mud and feces. Yet somehow, absurdly, this scene felt somehow fitting. It made a kind of sense, as if I was finally realizing my destiny, my self-fulfilling prophecy, my will to fail. I remember the motionless, nightmare-like fear of it—the tranquil, horrific stillness in this, the most terrifying moment of my life.

I began to imagine myself as his sex slave. I could feel my

soul breaking away from my body. I was giving what was left of my physical self over to him; I was becoming his vessel. The pain was the only thing keeping me from drowning in my own nonbeing.

Now, as I look into his terrified eyes down the muzzle of this gun I recall the astonished horror in my father's eyes as he gasped and fell to his knees in his studio. I watched as his eyes rolled back in his head, his mind drowning in the blood being released into his brain.
He loved you. Why did you do this horrible thing to him? Your own father! No, he hated me! *He loved you with everything he had. He loved you.* I didn't mean to hurt him. *Liar!* I didn't intend to destroy him.

He moaned in agony as he fell backwards to the floor. *You pushed him, you pushed him too far!* But he never came to my rescue. *And you killed him!* No! *Now, no one will ever come to your rescue.* I'M SORRY, PAPA! *You didn't deserve to be rescued.* PLEASE FORGIVE ME! *You killed the man in the white hat.*
But there is no man in the white hat.
Not for you. Because you're the Big Bully.
Yes.
You've lost!
Yes. Yes!
You are utterly beyond redemption.
I am.
You're alone! You've always been lost and alone.
YESSSS!
You will always be alone. Do this thing. Kill this man. Free yourself from your misery. It's the only way. Take him down with you! Do it NOW!
No!
Take action! ACT NOW!
I'm afraid.

Gusto starts to get up.
STOP HIM!
I remove my mask. Gusto stops. He looks at me, confused at first. Then, as if a light has clicked on in his head, he looks into my eyes and stops hard with a deep knowing. He remembers me! HE REMEMBERS ME!

The blood rushing to my cheeks emboldens me. I pull the hammer of the gun back into position and aim it squarely at his forehead. I scan the warehouse with my sensors. No one is watching. I *know*. I can feel it. I have a supreme knowing that comes with absolute power over another man's life.

"If you do this," he mumbles.

"SHUT UP!" My words echo like an indifferent thunder in the hellhole of a Nazi furnace. So this is what power feels like.

He held all the power back then, in his apartment. I wish I could have made him stop. *But you didn't.* He kept pushing himself in and out of me, his eyes rolling back in his head. Why couldn't he just stop? *He'll never stop. Because he is you. You have become your own predator. You are the hunted one, the slave, the fool. You brought this on yourself. You chose it. This is who you are, who you were meant to be!*

NO! He's committed crimes against humanity.

The pressure of each thrust was confirmation and punishment for every sin I'd ever committed. In that moment, thirty years ago, I was nothing more than a receptacle for his semen; it was clear that my only purpose in this wretched life was to be his slave, his fuck-pig, forever and ever, amen.

And you are still his slave. You chose this life. No! I was his prisoner. His victim.

My head is spinning now. I've got to get out of here. *STAY WHERE YOU ARE!*

All I remember was the overwhelming feeling of having to shit. I wanted to shit him out of me! *You couldn't.* I wanted to run away! *Where would you have gone? The door was locked.*

THE FISHFLY

I was afraid he wouldn't like me anymore, even after all that. *What if no one ever liked you again? What if you are fundamentally incapable of being liked?* No one ever liked me and they never will.

After he'd finished with me, he started speaking to the wall; there was no one there. He was talking to the wall. Later, he called the Vatican; he tried to get the pope on the phone. Was he fucking with my head or was he really insane?

None of that matters. Don't you get it? You've devoted your entire life to proving, over and over again, that you're the victim. You've negated every thought or feeling you've ever had that didn't fit the image of your self-loathing.

Who are you? I don't know this voice.

I am you. I'm all you have!

No, I'm alone. There's no one inside me. Just my thoughts.

You don't really believe that. You really believe these voices are separate from you.

NO!

We are you! I am your voice!

No.

You caused your father's stroke. It was because of you he's a vegetable!

NO. Stop.

It was your fault!

NO!

Yes, it was ALL your fault! Everything that's ever gone wrong in your life...all of it...it's all your fault! You provoked Kerry Fanning. You pushed Annie Sanders. You caused your father to have a stroke. You made your mother abandon you. You even encouraged Gusto to molest you. All to make yourself the victim. You are the source of all the wrongs ever perpetrated against you.

How can that be? All these terrible things couldn't have been my fault!

They were ALL your fault. All of them!

No, some things just happened to me!
It ALL just happened to you!
Yes, all of it happened to me!
You were there. You are the common denominator. Open your eyes and see the truth. You cast yourself as the victim in every case. You've cast everyone else as the perpetrator of your victimization. Your mother left you alone for a few hours; you chose to call it abandonment. Gusto simply seized the opportunity you gave him These are the stories of YOUR life. They are your creation. YOU ARE THE CAUSE OF YOUR STORIES.
Yes, I am the cause.
You gave the stories their meaning.
Yes, they're my stories, my meanings.
You have chosen to make yourself the victim, in every case.
But I was the victim!
BECAUSE YOU CHOSE TO GIVE OTHERS POWER OVER YOU! You have chosen the meaning of every story in your life! Things happen. Yes. But you have chosen what each experience means to you. Your stories are not actually real; they are only what you've chosen to believe about the events in your life. You have determined who you are based on a string of fallacious lies. But you are not your stories. TAKE RESPONSIBILITY FOR YOUR LIFE.
NO!
I squeeze the gun hard in my palm, extending my arm straight toward Gusto's face. His eyes widen. He begins to mutter, "I'm sorry, I'm sorry." He repeats this like a mantra, under his breath. Does he think he can ward me off with some pathetic play for mercy, as if he's suddenly the innocent one?
Don't give in to compassion. That's just another story, another lie. He'd say anything to save his miserable life. He has no remorse, no conscience—only fear. But his stories are not your stories.
But he deserves to die.

THE FISHFLY

He must be stopped!
I MUST KILL HIM TO BE FREE.
Must you?
Yes. I accept my life is empty and meaningless. My stories are hollow. But he must die for what he's done.
Perhaps.
He is evil.
But you have CHOSEN that he is evil. That you have made him evil has kept you enslaved to him for thirty years. This is what is true for you!
But evil must be stopped.
Then you must make the choice to stop it.
I have a choice?
Yes.
I can choose to stop evil?
Yes. And you can also choose the means. You get to say.
No, I'm—
You've always known this to be true. You are powerful. You are whole and complete.
I am whole and complete.
And you are nothing.
I'm nothing?
YOU ARE NOTHING.
Yes, I am nothing.
The voice of my nothingness echoes for a moment.
"Why did you do it?" I ask, hoarsely, looking into Gusto's frightened eyes. The sound of my actual voice startles me.
"It's who I am," he stammers.
"I've lived my whole life believing that what you did destroyed me."
"Did it?"
Rather than answer his question, I widen my stance and brace myself to fire the pistol into Gusto's face.
A fishfly flutters delicately into the light and lands on the sight at the tip of my gun. I stare at the audacious creature for

a long moment, into its tiny, primitive, God-like eyes. Its graceful, transparent wings glow in the dim light. I squint. From my perspective the fishfly is interposed directly in front of Gusto's head; they appear to be exactly the same size. We are all three, one.

I see my past, present and future with a simple clarity, as if for the first time. I feel a serene emptiness, a supreme acceptance.

There is a long, peaceful stillness and it is filled with silence.

Then more silence.

Finally, the fishfly flutters away and disappears into the darkness.

I lower the gun and replace the firing pin back into the safety position.

I listen.

More silence.

For the first time in my life, there are no voices in my head.

Slowly, I pick up my bag containing everything I own. I turn and walk out of the shadows, toward the sound of the few remaining revelers daring to celebrate Ash Wednesday on the streets of the Big Easy. I drop the gun into a trash bin, without missing a step. I walk. I keep walking, into the French Quarter, into my future.

-end-